Paperback ISBN: 979-8-9875277-0-2

eBook ISBN: 979-8-9875277-1-9

Publishing Assistance: Michelle Morrow, M.S.

Cover: Zooe Franci

Chapter Art: Zooe Franci

To my family, especially my husband, for all their support and help in making this Author dream of mine a reality. To the friends who encouraged me throughout this journey and kept pushing me to keep going. To E for all her time and wisdom.

To my kids, who I hope will always follow their dreams without the promise of success. To all the others who were much needed blessings on this journey.

Thank you for everything.

Author Note

A Sea of Blood and Tears is inspired by Norse and Celtic folklore and mythology. It is not intended as an accurate retelling of any specific myth. While parts of this story are inspired by real locations, all parts of this story are fictional and should not be taken as fact. This book is a work of fiction. All names, characters, events, and incidents are either a product of the author's imagination or used in a fictitious manner. Any resemblance to actual persons, living or dead, or actual events is purely coincidental.

ALSO BY

ALSO BY J.K DIVIA
Berja
A Witch's Penance
What The Sea Knows

Contents

Ionna

The Selkie Beach

1

NOT MY STORY

Only I know how you call to me,
the dark waters of my love,
the Sea.
Pull me down into your depths
and let me sleep there for eternity.
A happy Selkie I would be,
if my final rest could be with thee.

I draw the old patterns of my people in the damp sand beside me.

Loud, breathless giggles come crashing over the roaring of the waves and the songs of the seabirds. The gentle sea wind carries on its kisses the noise of clumsy childhood legs splashing in the water, along with the body of a dark grey seal crashing in the surf. It chases after my two children in a game of watery peek-a-boo. The happy bark of the seal meeting with the squeals of delight from the children creates a song of joy that sings directly to my heart.

As I watch them play, I get a sense of lightness; the joy they emit is contagious, and I am not immune. I soak in the light and warmth from overhead, a smile broadening across my face. The children are free in their nakedness, experiencing the joy of the warm sun against their bare skin as their clothing sits in a messy pile beside where I sit. I am also bare skinned, my dress pulled down to my waist as I enjoy the rare freedom to experience the sun's warm embrace along with them.

They run to me for mock safety during their game. With a gentle pat on their bottoms and a chorus of laughter so contagious that even the birds join in, I send them scurrying back to the shallow surf.

I watch her as she plays with my children. They are her kin, though not her people. Her sleek, dark grey skin is unmarked except for a light pink outline and the indentations of a wound from long ago. One that had healed in a way as to match her beauty, maybe even enhance it in certain light. Her glistening, dark, round eyes are an inky black pool that anyone would happily get lost in.

I often imagine what she would look like now without her coat. If her hair would be long and dark, wild like the waves in a fierce storm like our mother's had been. Tangled curls crashing into a beautiful pale face as the sea wind blows. Large dark eyes that match the shape of the moon at its fullest.

It's been so long since I have seen her without her coat; not since we were small children. Our grandmother would lead our colony to gather and celebrate under the seventh full moon of the seventh year, singing and dancing naked under the bright illumination coming from the night sky. Not since I caused the large scar that still so vividly marks my sister like a brand.

It's a constant reminder of the pain I caused her and our family. She wears my emblem of guilt with such grace. She could make anything look beautiful, even my mistakes. There are times when I desire nothing more than for her to leave me, as if her doing so would provide me comfort. To not face the visual markers of our childhood that had once anchored me until I found the strength to break free and come ashore. As I sit here on the beach and watch her play the sea games, her dark grey body slipping in and out of the waves, I am also terrified at the thought of that dark desire ever coming to pass.

"Eeeeee!!"

Aidan's squeal of delight interrupts my musings as Aine plants a stolen kiss once more on my son after sneaking up on him in the surf.

"Momma!" Aidan yells as he comes running over.

His little sister runs uncoordinated behind him, pumping her little arms with determination as she tries to keep up with her big brother. Tired from their game with their Aunt Aine, the children stumble onto my lap with heavy breaths, their tired legs giving out. Each of my thighs now bears a little head with damp, soft hair that smells like the Sea. Smiling, I lay a hand on each precious one and breathe in this perfect moment. The contrasting hair of the children, one dark and one light, now divides my lap.

Slipping up out of the waves, Aine comes bobbing up to sit near us. I wonder if her legs would also be as clumsy as mine. She comes to sit in the shallow surf, stopping at the boundary where the water no longer caresses the sand—a boundary that neither she, nor any of our kind, will cross anymore. Not since that night so many years ago when we were children, and I answered the call inside me that was always present. The one that pulled at me from the inside to wander to places I was not meant to be, no matter how hard I tried to ignore it. The one that led to Aine's scar. The one that ended the moon gathering cycle for the Selkies of our colony.

We sit here in the late afternoon sun, still basking in the warmth and happiness from moments ago. Perhaps sensing the children's need for rest, the clouds begin to gather once more in the sky above us, filtering the bright light and direct heat from the sun as they normally do.   I begin to hum an old song as I gently rock my upper body, my hips and bottom still planted firmly in the cool, damp sand. I sway with the rhythm of the waves and rub my children's heads as their fidgeting slows and they fight their heavy eyelids.

"Grandmother's song," Aine says with a soft, gentle bark before joining me in the lullaby.

Her dark grey body glistens in the sunlight that always finds her. She sways in rhythm with me, and my body buzzes with the joy of rare synchronization with my sister. Our duet makes me wonder how each of our voices would sound now in the other's form; if we would sound the same or not.

We sit here, the four of us, surrounded by the comforting sound of the Sea and the salty taste of the air we share. I am thankful for these moments, protected from the view of any of the villagers on the beach further down. A narrow barrier of tall sea grass and the rocky jetty that stretches down into the Sea feels like the protective arm of a parent, sheltering us from danger. Not that any of the villagers would dare come down this far, or near me.

This moment with my two youngest children in my lap and my sister beside me, surrounded by the Sea and protected from the village and what lies beyond, is almost all I could ever ask for. I want to soak it all up like the warmth of the sun that I can still feel on the skin of my children as I move my hands from their heads to their backs. The lightness in my heart continues to grow as I go back to lightly brushing the hair on the sweet faces of my babies. They are sleeping soundly, having lost the short battle with their eyelids.

"Ionna," Aine interrupts our song with a short, low bark, breaking our harmony and bringing me out of the blissful laziness of the moment.

I turn to look at her and am met with a hint of un-easiness in her large dark eyes, something I have rarely seen in her ever-confident face. She is still now as her upper half is raised tall out of the water, showing her lighter colored underside. She looks commanding in this posture, like the true leader she is. That she was always meant to be.

"It's time for you to come back," she continues.

My back involuntarily straightens, and my entire body goes stiff. My hands stop petting the children's hair and now covers their ears instead. They are used to the sounds of my people's language, though they do not understand most of it. I am unsure myself if I am covering their ears to protect them from the noise, or this conversation that Aine has started out of nowhere, tearing us out of this rare, fleeting happy moment. It has been a long time since any mention of me coming back was made. Not since after I lost Cael. I had thought we were safely far past this conversation.

"No."

"Ionna, it's time."

"No, I will never leave my children." I say, my face hardening against her words.

"You do not belong here." In a frustrated groan she continues, "Sooner or later you will have to come back."

"No, I won't."

"You don't have that choice anymore, Ionna. Something is coming!" Her shrill bark sends a cold shiver down my spine, and a wave of nausea builds in my stomach. I feel silly and angry with myself for getting lost in what has been the perfect morning and afternoon, and letting it go on for too long. Guilty for stealing myself into my children's happy moments like a suckerfish attaching itself to a whale. I should have known, should have expected it to come crashing down abruptly like this.

Her barks and groans have grown louder since she started this conversation, bringing our colony to gather further out ahead in the water. In tune with their matriarch, they have no doubt sensed her uneasiness and come to look for danger. Tiny dark heads bob in and out of the waves. I feel their eyes on us, and a tingling sensation begins to creep across my skin like a thousand pinpricks along with a flash of anger at being spectated by my family. I am no longer a part of the colony, but her tone affects me the same way, and every piece of me feels the anxiousness of being on high alert. I cover the children's ears a little heavier, causing Naia's dark head of hair to readjust on my lap.

"Nothing comes through the barrier, except us."

"Ionna, not yet doesn't mean not ever."

"No," I say again, shaking my head.

"The hunters came back yesterday, pushing through their catch. They heard a warning song carried across the currents from our cousins in the deep. They sang about a ship whose direction was headed this way. It was filled with devils from the land, filled with strange-ness, spears and bows. The front of the ship held a light that guided them; one they think could penetrate the mist."

"A human hunting ship, nothing else."

Naia stirs again, and I go back to stroking her hair and humming quietly again but am unable to make it as soothing as it was before.

"Ionna, this one is different. There is nothing else out there for them but this island, no reason for them to be out this way. The nearest land is a much further journey away. There is nowhere else for them to go but here, and they will be here soon. They will do what men on ships do. They will take, they will rape, and they will destroy before they leave."

Her aggravation is clear as she scoots one inch closer, placing a flipper across the boundary where the water ends before quickly moving it back across and reposturing herself. A misstep is so unlike her that it causes the queasiness to rise further up from my stomach to the bottom of my throat.

"Ionna, you cannot ignore what is coming."

"I will not leave my children."

"You must. Why is this so hard for you? Have you forgotten who you are entirely? Have you completely forgotten the call of the Sea? Are you so deaf now, you can no longer hear it? So numb you cannot feel it?"

"I have not forgotten, Aine. Though I have spent many nights wishing I could. Yes, it still calls to me, still pulls at me."

Raising my hands to gesture to my children, I say, "They call and pull to me more."

"You mean he does. Cael, the one you lost."

I look away from her, and my children stir uncomfortably from the hard changes in my body. The truth is much more complicated than what I have explained to her so far. I wish I could tell her more, in a way that could make her fully understand. If I could find the right words and beckon them to spill out, then maybe I could completely understand the truth myself.

"These children were never meant for you, Ionna."

"Lost is not gone; I will find him. Once the rest of the children are grown and safe."

"What about these children then, Ionna?"

"The ones who were never meant to be mine? I told you; I will stay with them until they are grown and safe. Since when does a Selkie care about leaving their coatless children behind? If I were to return to the Sea, as you are telling me to, their fate would be the same, regardless. If I leave them with the village, they'll abandon them the second they step onto the wrong piece of dirt. Abandonment is your solution to what is coming. Abandonment is what Selkies do to those who cannot follow."

"No, Ionna. Abandonment is what you did to us, to the Sea. I will never understand your reasons, even as you have tried to explain them. You don't have to let your pain anchor you to a life you were never meant to stay in. I love your children, Ionna. I love them as if they were my own."

"But," I say.

"But you belong in the Sea."

"Where they can't follow," I say.

"They belong to the land," she says in a way that is not meant to be cruel, just matter of fact.

"They belong to both," I say defiantly.

We sit here with silence between us. I uncover the children's ears and go back to softly stroking their heads with trembling hands, trying to soothe the light strains on their still-sleeping faces from the agitation of our conversation and rigidness of my body. Even the seabirds have fallen silent, as if the whole Sea is listening in on our conversation, waiting to hear what comes next. I want to ask what side they are on, but I know. They are all with the Sea.

Aine has never lost a child; she could never understand what she is asking of me. It's rare a Selkie mother here has, not since our ancestors followed the giant sea mist monster—the one who now sleeps after settling on the seabed of a drop-off miles offshore from here. Only two nostrils appearing as large craggy rocks remain unsubmerged. Its breath creates the dense mist barrier. Its misty breath locked out the dangers from the Sea that had plagued the previous Selkie Island and whelping sites. Only the Selkies know the way through. Only the dangers from the land remain here for us.

"What if they could?" Aine asks, breaking the silence, a sudden change in her tone catching me off guard.

"If you will not come back, if there was a way to send the children in your place, would you be willing to do it?" she asks after a long pause.

Confused, I turn back to look at her. Naia begins to stir before waking, moving to sit herself up. Grunting, she places a foot on her brother and tries to push him out of my lap as she slides in and wraps my one arm around her waist. I pull her gently back to the side of my lap as I continue stroking Aidan's light hair as he still sleeps. My chin comes to rest on the top of her dark wild hair as I begin to sway with her back and forth. She sleepily sucks her thumb in silence, leaning her entire body into mine.

"Do you remember the story grandmother used to tell?" Aine asks.

I don't reply, but I know the one she speaks of. How could I forget it? It is a story, a warning, passed down through the generations. One we all carry in us. Aine begins to tell the tale of the beautiful Selkie Maid, and I find myself unable to stop echoing her words in the tongue of my husband's people. Unable to keep myself from passing it to my daughter. A duty I had never planned to carry through. Though I never meant to share this with them, the words of it flow from Aine to me, and through me to my daughter's ears. The same way it has flowed from every Selkie Matriarch to Selkie Mothers and their sea-born children through the generations.

Naia sits quietly, still sucking her thumb, and I am unsure if she will understand, if she will be able to comprehend, if she is even fully awake. I hear my voice echoing as Aine continues the story.

"A daughter of the Sea who also loved the warmth of the sun. When the sun was high, and the day was clear, she couldn't resist laying on the warmth of a sunbaked rock without her coat. Sunning herself in such a way cost her everything. A cruel fisherman happened upon her one day, taking her coat by surprise. He was rough as tempest waves, and just as angry as the winds in such a storm.

"Every day since she lost herself, the beautiful Selkie maid would walk to the water's edge, tears streaming down her battered and bruised face. Every day, she would stand there and cry out for her mother. Cry out for the Sea. The waves would lap at her ankles. The water would lovingly pull the sand around her feet, causing her to sink a little more into it. It would pull the bottom of her rough linen dress back towards the Sea, beckoning her to return, though she was unable. Her family would gather in the water just past the wave breaks and listen to her cries, unable to help.

"Eventually the fisherman would come to fetch the maid. Collecting rocks and debris he found, he threw them at the seals bobbing in the water until all but one dispersed. The maid was left to cry under the watchful eye of the lone seal until her captor tired of his game.

"The young Selkie woman was forced to return to the village, where no love or kindness waited for her. Her mother, bobbing in the water watching and listening, was unable to bear the sadness and cruelty that had befallen her daughter any longer. The pain of watching her child was a weight she was unable to continue to carry.

"The maid had lost count of the days she spent walking down from the village to the water's edge. The days spent washing her wounds from the day and night before in the cold salt water. The mornings spent crying out, as had become her new life's ritual. When she saw her Selkie Mother walk out of the water, those days didn't matter anymore.

"The daughter didn't feel detached for the first time since being captured. The Mother went to her daughter, grabbing her battered face in her cool hands, chilled from the coldness of the Sea. She kissed her beautiful and broken child, stroking her dark, knotted hair and beaten face, gently and lovingly as a mother does. She took her daughter's hand, telling her to shed the cloth of her captor. Helping her daughter to undress from the rough fabric that imprisoned her, the mother tenderly dressed her daughter in her own coat, kissing the tears away from her face when they had finished.

"Naked in the morning sun, the mother only had left with her a whalebone knife that was as white and ominous as the old bones of sea giants that glow in the depths of the dark seabed. The mother cut open her hand, and then her daughter's. Now wrapped in her mother's skin, she sank into her arms and sobbed in both relief and sadness as her mother held her bleeding hand to her daughter's, letting their blood combine in a pool in their hands that began to stream down their embraced arms.

"Gently, the mother guided her sweet girl into the water, picking her up in both arms once again cradling her as a small child once they were waist deep. She rocked her in the waves of the Sea. Quietly, she sang a song whose words are long lost. The daughter lay her head on her mother's shoulder, eyes closed. As the mother sang, her daughter transformed once again into her true form.

"The mother rocked her daughter, now back to her seal form, in her arms a bit longer before releasing her. She stood silently and smiled as she watched her daughter roll under the waves and glide through the water free and weightless. The fisherman arrived at the beach in time to see his catch slip away and flew into a rage. The mother stood there, waist deep in the sea, looking only out at the open water peacefully.

"She did not acknowledge or fight when the fisherman confronted her. She didn't utter a sound when he grabbed a handful of her long, black hair, or make any attempt to escape as he pulled back her head and pressed the blade of the same whalebone knife she had used and then discarded earlier in the sand against her throat. He screamed at the Sea as seals bobbed in the water a few yards ahead, out of reach.

"The mother's blood was pulled out into deeper water by the waves, slowly dissipating. The fisherman was left with nothing, and the daughter, though returned, was not the same from what had befallen her. From what had been sacrificed for her. Every day since then, the fisherman's nets would always be empty, and his nights would be filled with the loud barking and the sad song of a lone dark seal."

"Momma?" Aidan says sleepily, waking as Aine and I finish the story, the mood of the day now somber. I am unsure how much, if any, of our story he heard.

"Yes, baby," I say, kissing his head as he sits up to snuggle beside Naia.

"I'm hungry."

"Let's go home then," I say and move them off my lap to stand up, shaking off my skirt and pulling my dress back up over my chest and arms.

Once I am properly clothed, I start dressing the children. Aidan lets me help him as Naia impatiently tries to dress herself.

"I can do it by *myself*," she says with a furrowed brow and perfect pout.

"Ionna," Aine barks softly.

Picking up a child in each arm after a failed attempt to straighten Naia's dress, I turn back to Aine. Her big dark eyes are staring at me, but I am unable to read them now.

"Do you think it could work?" I ask, once again biting the inside of my cheek.

"Could what work, Momma?" Aidan asks, placing his hands on each side of my face, trying to move my gaze from Aine to him, but I remain fixed on her.

She is still looking at us with her deep dark eyes. Looking as if she is considering the question echoed by Aidan carefully.

"No, but if you will not use your coat to save yourself, you should at least try to use it to save them," she says, and I feel as though I can sense a subtle change, a hint of sadness in the depths of the black pools of her eyes.

"Bye bye Auntie Aine." Aidan calls impatiently, abruptly ending the conversation as the crankiness from his hunger grows.

We turn back to face the hidden path back to the village. I take a few steps and turn back around to

Aine. She still sits in the same place in the surf, now cast in a shower of sun beams as the clouds appear to have broken above only her while the rest of us remain under their shadow.

"The story was one coat to one person."

Aine stares back at me before slipping quietly back under the waves, leaving me and the children alone on the beach.

As I turn back to the village with a child in each hand, I think about how there are moments in our lives that anchor us in them. That anchors us to the past. How sometimes these moments are ours, and sometimes they are inherited from our ancestors, like my Selkie ancestor from the story.

Occasionally, we can find ourselves able to break free from these moments. To move forward, if only for a bit. Find ourselves free from the weight of a moment we once thought as inescapable as an unbreakable chain. But all chains rust with time. You might find yourself able to break through, able to finally swim forward. You and those around you praise your strength as you do. No one realizes the toll it has taken, or how weak you have become, until it's too late. Until you find yourself anchored once again. Trapped in another moment. Tethered to another chain. One that is stronger, without rust.

Captured, forced, released. That is the story passed down through the generations. That is the story I have passed down to my daughter. I carried this story with me, in me, for the longest time. I can still feel the weight of the tether's cuff around me, still chafing. But I remind myself that I am not *that* Selkie maid. That it is not my story. I did break that chain. I did swim forward. I did leave the Sea on my own will, not forced.

But it didn't last long, the freedom. I once again find myself anchored, but this time the tether is tied to the land. This time there is no breaking free. Though I am not that Selkie maid, I hope that I can be the Selkie mother from Grandmothers story. I pray that I can save my children.

BJORN

THE SHIP

2

OF BEARS AND MEN

"Tell me, who here is afraid of death?"

"Not I!"

"Was that a whisper on the wind? Tell me, who is afraid of death?!"

"Not I!!" The shouts of the men beat out against the sea wind like a drum.

The men who kneel before him are weak things. They don't understand how easily their bones break and their blood flows between the powerful claws and sharp teeth of my brothers and I. There was a time I thirsted for the crunch of bones and salt of blood of his enemies. There are times even now when Anders brings out the blood lust in me, though I am forced to fight alongside him now.

The men, not brothers, kneel before him. Anders is the leader of the men under Einar. The ones we were forced to recruit to fill the empty space of the dead brothers on our ship and ranks. The ones lost in the pursuit of a better world for men. Their faces look up and necks are outstretched, chests laid bare and inviting.

They welcome death in bravery. To buy their entrance to Valhalla, where they will sing and feast and await the great battle. It seems a wasteful thing, to spend time dreaming of feasts that will never come to be while so many of them starve. They think they are brave, but I can hear the beat of their hearts, the quickening of their pulse in this moment as they believe in the truth of this mock test.

"Look, here they come. The great bear warriors. The ones who think they are better, stronger, and braver than you," he says with a sly smile, pointing his blade towards me and Mads as we come closer to where the men are lined up before him.

"But we know the truth, all beasts are afraid of death, they can't help it. It's not their fault. All animals are afraid to die. We are better than animals, we are braver than bears. This is why the gods prefer the blood of men over beasts. Who is afraid to die, men?"

I can hear Mads' booming laughter behind me as anger rises within me. These men who idealize death but don't know the cost. Who don't bear the cost of death. Whose sacrifices do nothing but lessen the mouths they struggle to feed. Mads places his hand on my shoulder as the hair begins to rise on my body.

"I am not afraid to die. I am a man of Norge!" A smaller man with long blonde hair stands up. It's always the smaller ones with something to prove. Anders smiles as he walks over to the now-standing man.

"Yes, brother," Anders says as he walks to the man, standing in front of him and placing his forehead against his before pulling back and slitting the man's throat.

"This is a man of Norge," Anders says, raising both his arms up to the sky, knife dripping in blood in one hand. "This is what the glory of death looks like. Until we meet again in Valhalla, brother."

"In Valhalla," the rest of the kneeling men say.

I stare at the man as his body quivers, his red blood draining out on the weathered planks of the ships deck. They all look the same when they die—faces with various degrees of shock or confusion. Their faces all blend together, as do their deaths.

"Watch your step Bjorn," Anders says as we near the still-moving body of the man on the ground. "I know how much you hate getting blood on your hands."

The bear within me emerges at his words, and the first flow of blood and crunch of bones enters my mouth, before I feel a sharp pain in my head and fall to blackness.

EINAR

THE SHIP

3

FRUIT OF OUR FATHERS

"You need to eat more."

"I'll not suffer the rations of a dead man."

"You're weak."

"Not as weak as the faith of your men in the face of a mild sea storm."

"The dead man may argue it is stronger."

She pulls a white blanket with intricate gold and deep blue thread around her frail figure tighter as she huddles further away from me. It was a gift I had presented her with at the start of our journey. Her deteriorating condition matches that of the worn, red wool cushion she sits upon. They had both been so vibrant when we first set out. Before the elements and exertion of the loads they carry began to take their toll.

The ship heaves once more, and an apple rolls off the table and along the floor, no doubt adding to the bruises it already bore.

"There was time, I am told, when the tables of our fathers before us overflowed with the choicest of meats and fruit," I say.

She doesn't look up at me as I retrieve the fallen fruit or accept the imperfect offering from my outstretched hand.

"The problem with a land already spoiled is there is never enough. Those left unsatisfied are always a threat. The bruises will always deepen, and eventually rot us to our core. Eat, you need your strength." I say again gently, raising my empty hand to place on her golden head.

"You mean you need my strength." She says.

"I need more than that," I bite off one of the bruises on the apple and offer it to her once more. "I need that virgin land who waits for my will to lay it seeded and sown."

I force my touch to leave her and head towards the men waiting outside my tent. The storm is abating, and there is the blood to wash clean and my will to ensure. As I reach the threshold I call back, "You will be there with me. You are the beacon that lights the way for those who are ready to set foot upon our new world. Your light will guide me the entire way."

Ionna

The Village

4

HOW DO YOU CHOOSE

There is no safety of a rookery here.

I gently pick up Naia and place her in a woven basket lined with scraps of cloth and raw wool. There are no other sea mothers to keep a careful watch for danger while I am temporarily gone. I carefully tuck the old woven basket with my precious catch in the corner, where she will be safely hidden. A wild curl behind her ear refuses to be tamed and falls upon her soft, sleeping face. It is soft under my fingertips as I start to move it behind her ear, then stop. Why shouldn't it be free? It did not grow to rest easy or be tucked away.

The mothers in the village carry their children with them in slings made of cloth. I cannot take her with me, though. My lips brush against the soft skin of her chubby cheek and I breathe in the salty scent of the Sea that still lingers on her skin from yesterday. What I believe was our last perfect day at the beach before

Aine broke the news that our world as we know it will be ending. My lips move to her nose for one last kiss before I go. The kisses we share in this form are ending. She lets out a sigh and nestles down into the basket. She doesn't know our time left together will be brief.

"I love you, my sweet child." I whisper as I lay the woven lid with its rips and holes upon the old basket to further conceal her as best I can.

"I will be back soon. I promise."

I move as slowly as the receding tide away from her, forcing myself to move towards the door, and to the secret Selkie Beach path behind our hut.

The light grey-brown sand is still cool under my feet, not yet warmed by the mid-morning sun. My husband and our boys are out in the village to trade the early morning's catch. They won't be back until early evening, leaving me enough time to see Aine and get back before Naia wakes from her nap, before the boys return home.

I walk quickly down the path, counting one footstep after the other, trying to slow my heartbeat to match them. This is the only path on the entire island that has ever brought me joy. It is the one that leads me to the precious moments with my children and their sea family. The coolness of the rocks help steady me as I move quicker down the path until the feeling is lost into emptiness. I stop and almost fall forward from the gap in the rocks at my side. To the entrance of a place that once contained all my joy.

The wind blows gently on the path, lifting my hair and echoing my Daithí's words from years ago. I can feel the weight of his last whispers from then echoing in my ear.

"Tell me a story, my Love."

His dark head raises slightly from where it rests on my chest. His forearm drapes across me. The warmth of the sun beats down from above. It combines with the warmth of our entangled bodies, enhancing this moment of bliss. Our secret nest of sea grass and crumpled clothing, discarded in a rush, provides us with a comfort not found at home.

It offers a sense of safety from the reality of the world beyond the protection of our rocky sanctuary. Free from the entanglement of nets weighed down by expectations, responsibilities and the past. Free from the sharp spear tips of judgement that always seem to be pointed in my direction, ready to wound me. Nothing can touch us here. He breathes in time with the waves beyond our shelter, steady and strong. The world outside this perfect moment can wait a little longer.

He cranes his neck up to offer me a kiss.

"I only know of one."

"Tell me."

Remaining quiet after a long kiss, he nuzzles his head back down, placing it between the warmth of my growing breasts and belly. The warmth of the sun and our entangled bodies put me in a state of bliss. I playfully tug at his coarse, dark hair, alternating between teasing it and smoothing it back down.

"Tell me." I say again.

"A beautiful Selkie Maid, who loved a poor, dark haired village man as much as she loved the warmth of the sun." He starts out with a playful squeeze of my breast. "She lay with her lover, who was the most handsome."

Moving his body on top of mine, he begins to lightly kiss me, starting below my belly and moving up. My breath catches and giddiness builds. I start to laugh loudly in the direction of the sun. Carelessly. Recklessly.

"Is that so?" I say.

"Mmmm hmmm."

"Her lover begged her," he continues, his lips tracing a line to my breasts, "to run away with him." He brings his eyes to meet mine. "Run away with me."

"What?"

"Let's run away, Ionna."

I push him over to lay beside me and turn to snuggle in tightly against his warm body. Snuggling my face into his shoulder so his chin rests on top of my head, I evade his question. His lips press down on the top of my head as I pull his arm over me into an embrace. He lets out a deep sigh.

"At least let me get your coat back for you. Let me get you your freedom."

I pull his arm tighter around me, as if it could smother the secret fire burning inside me. It is fueled by the worry, fear, and shame that I can never seem to unload since our lips first met, that continues to dry me out, making the cracks and sores more visible. How do I explain how I came to be here and why I can never leave? What if he finds out the truth? I worry what he will think when he does. Panic mixed with relief sets in as we are interrupted by the sound of footsteps running down the path outside our hidden spot. We both rush to get dressed. Pulling my dress on over my head I hear, "Mama?".

Mama is all that I am now. No longer a lover, no longer a true wife. The gap in the rocks hides the once secret nest where I became a mama to Naia. Naia, who I must hurry back to. I urge my feet to carry me swiftly once more down the path towards my sister. I try to shake the memories of long ago, and what might have been had I taken Daithí's offer. An offer that saw me end my relationship with him rather than bear the heartache of him seeing me as I really was, as I really am.

The sand is warm where the sun beats down upon it freely, without obstruction from the rocks and mounds of seagrass that protect the path leading from my husband's cottage. It contrasts with the cool water that hits my toes and welcomes me to come further into its reach.

"Aine, please!"

The water greedily pulls at my skirt, and I reward it, walking until the waves hit my waist. Spray splashes my face. Reaching, pleading with arms and hands outstretched, I yell at her, "Help me!"

The water pulls back, taking with it my wet dress that tangles between my legs. I do not brace myself, and a wave crashes over me. I yell again as I am pushed under the water. My head hits the hard sand floor. As the sand from my fall combines with the water, my vision blurs. I struggle to stand up in this body that is anchored by these clothes. Finally, her head appears as we both surface.

"Aine!" But she disappears back down.

I slap the water in frustration and anger at being trapped in a body that can't move with the water as it once did. Water shoots painfully up my nose as I am knocked back under again. A broken shell cuts into my foot as I struggle once more to stand up. I feel her sleek, cold body brush against mine, encouraging me to shed what weighs me down and move with her past the breakers.

Her large, dark eyes bring me comfort after we reach the gentle rocking of the waves past the wave breaks.

"Aine." I gather my thoughts and my breath. "I only have one, what do I do?"

"You find a way to turn it into three, or you choose one."

Her quiet, soothing barking does nothing to lessen the horror and anger I feel at her. At her answer. I scream and cry out at the Sea, ripping my hair. I beat my chest, taking in the salty water until I can barely stay above it. The thought becomes alluring. I lay my head back, and the cold water covers my ears. Only my nose and mouth remain above.

I can hear the pounding of the Sea's heart, of Aine's heart. I can hear the hearts of the Sea mothers and their children beating in tune, and it's a welcome lullaby. I want to relax into the sound of their beating pulses, but my own heart interrupts the rhythm. It no longer beats in tune. I focus harder on the lullaby, but my heart's own rhythm reminds me I cannot hear my own children's hearts. I lift my head out of the water and bring my toes back to brushing the sandy bottom.

A row of tiny, dark heads appear out in the water a safe distance away, drawn by the noise of my tantrum, and I hate them for it. She didn't leave my side; she didn't move at all. She remains beside me, bobbing in the waves and weathering the fit of rage and emotion that has finally subsided in me. I stand limply in the water, letting the waves rock and soothe me from the storm that had just passed. The Sea whispered a promise to always catch me should I return, should I fall. I want to succumb once more to the sinking feeling inside me. The tiny dark eyes of the Sea children staring at me from a distance remind me of what is lost if I do not push through.

"How do you choose one child over another?"

"I don't know," she grunts back honestly.

"I guess you choose the one who needs you the most. Or you don't choose at all." The quiet barking of her voice is filled with sympathy that I know is true.

"What do you mean?"

"Your best chance of this working is to choose one child; we all know which one has the best chance of it working on. Or you find a way to turn your coat into three, which may lessen your odds of success. You could also do nothing, and return to us by yourself."

"No."

"Then you do the best you can. Make a decision. I can't promise it will be enough or that it will be right, but you need to do it soon, you are running out of time." The weight of her head on my shoulder is comforting as we rock together in the waves.

"The ship still approaches, sister. It won't be long now." The weight on my shoulder is gone as she swims around and placcs her forehead against mine briefly before slipping back under and out to the deeper water. I am left alone.

I linger for a moment, naked in the cold water before returning to the beach. I don't bother looking for the clothes I have shed in the water. The dry sand sticks to my wet feet as I make my way from the beach back up the path. I know I must find a way to make the three coats. I pick up my pace and hope Naia will still be sleeping when I make it back to the hut.

Aine would never leave her child alone on land like I did. She would never leave the Sea, would never cross that boundary. She would never be caught off guard sunning herself. A matriarch would never entertain the idea of leaving for a devil on the land like I did.

It has been a long time since I have been that far into the water. The Sea has never stopped calling me back to it and my family. There have been moments where I almost did answer its call. In those early years, there were a million times I thought to ask my husband to burn my coat or throw it away. At first to prove my love and devotion, and to remove the threat of temptation in a moment of weakness or sorrow, should I lay eyes upon it. Then, as a punishment.

As I force myself to move further up the secret Selkie Beach path, I am now grateful for the weakness that prevented me from having it destroyed. The weakness has provided me a chance to save my children. The softness of the path becomes rougher as the rocks and pebbles grow in number and I get closer to the entrance to our home. The cut from the shell stings the bottom of my foot painfully as I feel the jabs from sharp pebbles along the path. They serve as a warning, a reminder of the pain to come. A cut of this flesh will be nothing compared to the cut of my Selkie coat.

I hear nothing as I emerge from the path and walk the short distance to where I left Naia. I open the door to see my husband and children sitting silently at our table, the one made from old driftwood cast out by the Sea. Three small faces with lips stained purple and red from fresh berries look up at me. I see the outline of where a fourth should be. When the time comes, if I am able, I will cross the barrier to find my son, Cael. Once my other children are safely in the Sea, I will find him or face the same fate as him. I must find a way to make these coats.

"Momma, berries!" Naia squeals in delight as she throws up a berry-stained hand to show me.

My heart stops, and I know that I am caught. My plan failed. I wait for Cian to turn around, to scold me.

"Where are your clothes?" Caden asks with a raised brow and hard-lined mouth that mirrors his father's looks.

Naia and Aidan giggle and continue eating their treat with purple and red stained hands and mouths.

"No, Naia. These are just for us. We all have jobs to do, and the berries are only for those who do their jobs," my husband says.

He doesn't turn to face me. He doesn't comment on my lack of dress. He has long stopped asking or caring about my state or daily comings and goings.

"Cian." I cross the threshold into our small home, the sand falling off me and leaving a trail.

"We all have jobs, Ionna."

His indifference no longer stings. I know he is right; we all have jobs. I must convince him to help me with mine. What he lacks in love for me, he more than makes up for in his love for our children. I must find a way to convince him that sending them away is the only way to save them. Unlike the son we lost, we must do everything we can to get these children to cross the barrier into the Selkie world.

Ionna

The Village

5

JUST A GIRL WITH JUST A COAT

Last night was uneasy, as it so often is lying next to my husband in our cold bed. Only the warmth from the children as they climb in one by one during the night offers relief from the estrangement. Cian would not look at me, would not speak to me after they had finished their dinner. Only Naia, Aidan and I remain in bed now.

The silence continues into the morning as he and Caden get up together. Caden matches his father more and more lately in his disdain for me. "Why can't you be like the other wives?" is followed by "why you can't be like the other mothers?" The latter wounds me far more deeply than I thought possible.

If he only could see that I have tried. That my Selkie blood is a difference that could benefit him if he did not reject it so. That there is beauty and power in our strangeness. The fire in our hearth is burning strong after Cian stoked it this morning with Naia's basket. As if destroying it will prevent me from finding another place to keep her safely hidden when need be. I can hear him outside, unloading and cleaning up after this morning's fishing. I sit up slowly and gently wake the children.

"Come on my loves, let's go to the beach and see your Sea family."

Aidan sits up with a sleepy smile before diving into my lap and closing his eyes once more. I kiss his face and shake his foot until he starts to giggle and sits up in excitement.

"Go on and eat, there are berries left on the table and some bread. We'll go down when you are finished."

He races over to the table, grabs a handful of blueberries, and brings them back, offering some to me. I shake my head no and send him back to the table.

"Come on Naia," I say with a kiss and a nuzzle.

She finally wakes after some prodding, and I carry her to the table, sitting her next to Aidan while I grab dried fish for myself.

After we are finished eating, I hurry the children out the door and down the Selkie Beach path, avoiding my husband, who is preparing the fish to preserve.

The children run down the path, racing each other and laughing along the way. Their laughter echoes against the rocks. I will miss hearing it; I know deep down my husband will too. I know he blames me for Cael's loss as much as I blame him. He will no doubt blame me for sending our children to the sea as well. Even if it's to save their lives. I want to believe he will choose their lives, even a life separated from us, over certain death. I wish I could count on that. I wish he had chosen that for Cael.

The children strip off their clothes and throw them to the wind at the bottom of the path, rushing forward into the surf as Aine and some of her pups eagerly await them in the water. I know they are safe; no one comes down this path or to this sheltered beach but us. It's as close to a rookery as I can provide for my children. I take a moment to soak in their squeals and splashes before heading back up the path. I hope my plan will work. I hope they will remember these moments, these days they had with us in these bodies as they thrive in the Sea in their Selkie forms. Aine barks at me loudly from the surf, letting me know she will take care of them and urging me to move quickly with my task.

"Cian!" I call as I walk from the path towards our hut, stopping a few feet behind where he is crouched, working on untangling the nets from his early morning trip.

A small part of me has always desired to tell him that my family is the reason his nets are full, but I know he would not believe me, and it would not benefit our children to start such an argument. I struggle with where to begin with him. How do I start? I take another deep breath and begin.

"Cian, something is coming. My sisters..." I begin again, grabbing the sides of my dress with sweaty palms, "they're saying something is on the way. They're not sure what yet. But our cousins in the deep, they say men in a boat are coming. Heading towards the mist. They carry weapons and talk of the island. Talk of the wood."

The words spill out much faster than I intended. I find the courage to look at him, pleading with him to listen to me. But he continues to untangle the nets, not acknowledging my presence.

"Cia.."

"Da, can I go to the fields and help with the shearing?' Caden asks as he comes running up to us, cutting me off as he pushes his dirty blonde hair back from his eyes.

"Looks like the sheep aren't the only ones who need shearing." A genuine smile broadens across Cian's face as he turns around and beams at our son, like he so often does when looking upon our sons, especially Caden.

"We should stay close to home right now," I say.

Finally turning to look at me, he asks, "and where are Aidan and Naia just now, Ionna?"

"They're at the beach, with Aine."

"Oh yes.. I reckon that is a safe place for them to be with all this danger afoot, no?" he says with a wink to my son, causing Caden to smirk and a smile to creep back to his own face.

"They *are* safe with her."

"Yes, of course. Should monsters of the deep appear, or worse, a rogue wave, I'm sure a lone Seal is more than capable of keeping our two youngest safe."

Waving me off, he returns to the nets.

"Go on and head to the fields, boy. Show those village boys what hard work looks like."

Caden takes off running up the path towards the village with a beaming smile before I have a chance to utter another protest.

"Something *is* coming."

"The only danger to this family that has come from the sea in many years has been you, Ionna."

"That's not fair."

"Is it not?"

Dropping the nets forcefully on the ground and turning back to me he says, "Tell me then, what exactly is coming?"

One hand resting on his leg, he gestures towards the sea. "How will it get through the mist?"

I stare at him in silence, unable to share the secret of my people, anger threatening to spill out of me in my own tongue.

"Nothing comes through the mist. Nothing comes from the sea."

"I came."

"Did you now?" he asks, annoyance turning to anger.

"See, I've been hearing talk since you came that you washed up from the barrier somehow. I'm starting to think it's true. Who ever heard of a Selkie willingly give up their coat?"

His finger points at me as his words turn aggressive. "I never saw you transform. You just appeared with a coat, claiming you were one. Before there hadn't been a Selkie sighting since before I was a boy."

"You saw me," I counter. "You saw me before I took off my coat, and you know it. You lured me here, sang to me, gave me gifts of fish."

My voice begins to grow louder, my arms no longer locked at my sides as I speak. They flow freely with my words as I stand up to him in a way in which I have not done in many years. In a way that had just not seemed worth it for so long. He looks at me silently for a minute, as if considering my words. As if recalling the memory from so long ago. Despite the small release of tension from my outburst of words and movement, it still largely remains in my face and body, giving me a headache. I hope that he will remember, see that the words I speak are true and finally listen to me.

It feels like an eternity, waiting for him to speak again.

He drops his hands to his side; his face looks pained, tired as he speaks. I can see how the years have so clearly marked him in this moment. The sunlight betrays the glinting grey hairs that hide so adeptly in his dirty blonde hair.

"I was a damned fool to take you in. To believe your story," he says, his voice now low and with eyes that brim with tears. "You made me feel like I was special."

Those words wound me, and tears threaten my own eyes at his admission. He pauses for a moment, biting his lips.

"I wanted to believe that I was special. That I was more than this village. But I was wrong. I'm not special," he continues, "I'm cursed. I don't know what I did to deserve you. I keep waiting for the moment when whatever evil deed I must have done is absolved.

The moment when life and happiness will finally shine down upon me."

He takes a long pause, putting his thumb and pointer finger to the bridge of his nose.

Taking a deep breath and dropping his hand back down he says, "the only happiness I've been given has been those children. Especially Caden."

"What about Cael?" I ask.

Pointing towards the village he says, "Caden's been working hard to prove himself to the village. To be accepted by them."

Pointing his finger now back towards me, "I'll not have you ruin all his hard work with this talk of danger nonsense. Or getting in his way when his hard work finally pays off and he finally starts getting invited to join the other boys and men. He is redeeming this family. That boy alone is bringing us back into the village."

Taking a step towards me he says, "I'm warning you, Ionna. Do not get in his way."

He drops his finger and takes a step back towards the nets. "He has the first real chance to be happy, to be normal."

Before he turns his back to me, he says, "As his mother, I would expect you to want that for him as well. To not have to live with the burdens of being an outcast, of being rejected, unwanted. Being viewed as less than because of the blood and strangeness he carries within him—your blood, Ionna."

His words continue to wound. Of course, I do not want my children to be hurt, to bear the burdens of being outcasts. I want to protect them from that pain. Pain that I helped cause by bringing them here, to be trapped between two worlds. But they are my children. My blood runs through them, and my blood is important. My blood is their only hope.

"I am a Selkie." I stand up, unwilling to be pushed down with shame at this. "Our children are part of the Sea. You can't deny them their blood!"

"Oh? But isn't that exactly what you did?" His response catches me off guard. He always knows exactly where to stick the sharp spear tip of his words to cause the most pain. I stand there as his words begin to weigh me back down.

"I'm not special any more than you're a Selkie, Ionna. Though I can't say I believe you're a demon from the wood, either; not given the children you birthed. No monster could have created such wonders, not even one such as you. No, I know exactly what you are."

"And what is that?" I say.

"You're just a girl, with just an ugly coat."

"Something is coming."

"You'll say nothing to anyone about what is coming," he says sternly.

"I need a needle."

"It's a little too late to start being a proper wife now."

"Please?"

"I can't afford losing the one I have. You don't know how to use it, anyways."

"Teach me?" I crouch down and place my hand gently on his arm. Pleading.

"With what time, Ionna? The housework? The providing for our children so they can eat? That all falls on me while you are off wandering gods know where." He pulls his arm away from my touch.

He never seems to notice the things I do. He's not completely wrong, though. Gone are the days I spent our mornings collecting Sea grass while playing on the beach and in the tide pools with the children. Gone are the days when I would prepare my husband lunch. Meals of dried fish, bread and dulse from the dried red sea lettuce that my Cael had helped me harvest earlier in the week.

I tried so hard to make my husband happy then, to be a good human wife. It was my sole mission. I thought my happiness hinged on his back then. Why did I think that? I wish I had an answer. My son would still be here if I hadn't. I would still be able to eat the red sea lettuce. He would still be able to help me harvest it.

"If you find you have spare time, then watch our children yourself instead of leaving them under the care of the seals and the sea. Sorry, your family, as you say. More like under the care of poor Aidan, who you've left to do all the mothering instead of going with Caden to the fields and village."

I am numb from the emotional toll from fighting with him. From the words left unspoken for years that have finally emerged, leaving me drained. I have no more fight left with him.

"My coat," I say. "Where is it?"

IONNA

THE VILLAGE

6

HOW MUCH SALT IS ENOUGH

"Why?" he asks me.

"To save our children from what is coming."

"By abandoning them and returning to the sea?"

"You said you didn't believe me, that it's just a coat. Just a common animal hide, so what does it matter?"

He stares at me from where he remains crouched on the ground with the nets. Considering my words and his own from moments before, he looks away, then silently stands and walks towards the hut. I do not follow; I don't want to know how close it was to me all these years.

As I wait, I think about the few Selkies before me who stood between their children and the Sea, coat in hand. The ones who had to make a choice to stay or return, as I will. According to Aine, there is never a choice when it comes to the Sea or leaving it. I know that is true for most of my kind.

I think about the children who were left behind, and wonder if they understood the pain their mothers were in. I worry about the children who will be leaving me, and if they will understand the pain I went through and what it meant to save them. Will their pain and sense of loss be the same?

I bite my cheek and taste the saltiness of the blood that flows in my mouth. I think about those children, lost through the generations. The ones still left with traces of the Sea in their blood, who felt a strange pull that they couldn't explain. I worry how much salt is enough, how much is too little. There is only one in the village who could understand us, a forgotten child descended from the Sea.

Daithí's Selkie blood slept quietly in his family's line for generations until he was born. Strange and quiet, he was clearly drawn to the Sea. A sense of melancholy always surrounds him, the result of inherited pain that was passed down through the generations from the unwilling Selkie in his bloodline to him. As near as I could tell, he has never tried to fit in as I did at first. He just exists as himself, and the village accepts him, unlike me, unlike my children. Except for maybe Caden, who apparently has been making great strides.

There are a few others who have come from the union of a Selkie and villager, but the salt in their blood is so watered down that they blend in seamlessly with the rest of the village. I can barely sense them myself.

The occasion when one of their people would find themselves in possession of one of ours has always been a rare occurrence. It would always end in heartbreak for both when it did happen. Most encounters were brief, and children were not always born from such meetings of our kind. It is well known that if a Selkie ever regains their coat, the call back to the Sea will be too strong for them to resist; even stronger than the call of the men or women that they had come to love. Stronger than the call of any children they may be leaving behind.

They would don their coat, their true skin, and return to the Sea. They would never again return to the land. Never again take off their coat. Others who had been caught would still make their way back to the Sea. In heartbreak and desperation, they would go without their coats to end their lives in the water. Selkies do not end their days at peace on land. Eventually, we always end up back in the Sea. Some sooner than others. I left the Sea as one. I pray that three will return in my place. I pray that the salt in their blood will be enough. It must be enough.

He returns with the dark grey leather of my skin in his hands. I instantly feel the pain of its dried-out state from years of being stored without water, without the sea. I rush forward, grabbing it from him and shocking us both with the aggressiveness of my movements.

"Go then," he says.

I want to. Every ounce of my body wants to go. To run down the path until the sharp grey pebbles give way to soft grey-brown sand and my body becomes one with my coat and the Sea. I can feel his pale blue eyes on me, and they seem curious again. Like they had been so many years ago.

"A needle," I croak.

He looks at me and seems disappointed I have not run towards the path to the Sea.

"What are you going to do?"

"Save our children."

"With that?"

"Yes," I say through gritted teeth.

He laughs and shakes his head.

"I told you," he says walking back towards the nets, "I can't afford to waste one on you."

I am left standing as every ounce of my body continues to scream and fight against me and my will to not return to the Sea.

"And you won't be taking the children anywhere. So run back to the sea if it'll have you."

I force myself to move away from where Cian stands, his back now turned towards me, and place my back firmly in the direction of the Selkie Beach path. Once again, he stands in the way of me saving our children. I can do this without him. I won't let him stand in my way again. As I force myself in the direction of the main village, I hear him mutter, "I knew you were just a girl."

Ionna

The Village

7

— · —

A NEEDLE TO SEW APART THE PIECES OF ME

One step. One foot out the door.

Two steps, and two feet planted in opposite directions in the dry rough earth outside our hut and away from my husband.

Three steps, and two feet turned forcibly in the wrong direction of the overwhelming desire I hold in my hands. Away from the path that leads to the Sea. Away from the only thing capable of quenching this thirst. How long has it been since I've touched my dark grey skin? Not since I left the Sea those many years ago.

Four steps, and I don't even feel the tiny stones that I know must be digging into my bare feet as I walk the path towards the village. I wish that I could. I wish that I could focus on the pain they should be causing me instead of the pain of fighting against myself. Against my nature. My hands are bone white as I hold it forcibly in front of my body. Every part of me buzzes. My insides scream so hard to be reunited with my skin that my bones ache, threatening to break.

I catch it pulling towards me as we reach out for each other. No! I move it further in front of me. My fingers fight me to break the lock of my grip and slither their way into an opening. Just one little slip under and it will overtake me. I am bare, raw and bleeding without my skin. Unprotected. Just one little slip and I could be back in it. The physical pain, the yearning caused by the separation that is only inches from ending, would stop.

Twenty steps towards the town. How could I forget what this would feel like? To hold my skin again. Why wasn't I prepared for this? I am no longer buzzing. I am burning.

Twenty-five steps. *You can't do this.* The heat of a thousand suns is burning my skin. It feels like I am covered in a thousand tiny blisters that are all threatening to burst at the same time. I am dying a thousand deaths in this moment. There is no end or beginning as the need and pain continue to peak and peak again.

Twenty-seven steps. Again

Twenty-eight steps. And again. I can't stop. I can't hesitate a single step. If I do, it's all over.

Twenty-nine steps. Cael. Caden. Aidan. Naia. Cael. I say their names over and over again. A mantra to get me through. *You couldn't save Cael, you can't save them.* CAEL. CADEN. AIDAN. NAIA. YOU CAN'T SAVE THEM! CADEN! AIDAN. NAIA!

Thirty steps. *You don't deserve them.*

Thirty-one steps. *They are better off without you.*

Thirty-two steps. *You don't belong here.*

Thirty-three steps. *You belong in the Sea.*

Thirty-four steps. Pain is temporary, I try to convince myself. But I know that it is a lie. Cael. Caden. Aidan. Naia. I say their names again. With Cael's name, I am reminded that some pain is permanent. I fight my Selkie blood every step of the way. Cael. I belong at the barrier with Cael.

The barrier is where I will end my days. Not the Sea. Not in my coat. Not with my other children, who will grow free and safe in the Sea with my family. I try to push the sensation of being burned alive out of my head and focus on the barrier. Focus on remembering why I am here. Why I am doing this walk. Focus...

My husband was working his turn with the others maintaining the barrier between the village and what lies beyond the dark wood line on the other side. He had never explained the barrier, a stretch of barren land wide enough for two small fishing boats to pass side by side on its dry bed of salted earth. He said only that it offers the village protection from what lies beyond, and to never cross it. That I needn't know more than that. That a husband's word ought to be enough for his wife.

It is barren because of the work the villagers do to lay salt harvested from the sea to kill any plants or life between the village and the woods. A short ground wall the height of a fisherman's basket clearly marks the boundaries on either side. I never thought to ask more about it. The ways of men are strange, and I learned to stop questioning my husband on them not long after I came. I preferred to spend my time close to the Ocean side, down by the beach anyways. Our son had just mastered walking, something my husband would tease that I still failed to do properly.

One hundred and two steps. Each step is excruciating, but these are not the hardest steps, the most painful steps of my life, no. The most painful steps were at the barrier that day. They belonged to my son. My Selkie skin wants to push all thoughts away that aren't of it, but I refuse. I cling to the pain now, to my reasons for taking this walk. I focus on our last morning together. On his face, and his giggle.

I didn't steal enough looks at my son while he slept, while he smiled as he dreamed. I was loading food into a woven basket and strapping it to my back as he began to stir. Helping him to wake up with kisses and smiles, I picked him up for those last sleepy snuggles. I put him in the sling across my chest that we both loved so much. It had been a gift from my husband. The soft, oat-colored cloth held him snuggly to my chest while I took us places too far for him to walk. When we got there, I waved my one arm vigorously above my head to get my husband's attention, making my boy giggle as I shook us both.

One hundred eighty-nine steps. How many steps down the muddy dirt path was it to the barrier? I wish I knew. I haven't been back since that day. I doubt I'll have time to count when I return. I replay that day in my head over and over again as it wins more ground over my skin.

"Cian!" I'd called.

He looked up briefly with a furrowed brow, lips in a hard, disapproving line before returning his gaze back down to his work. Why wasn't he answering me? I was confused and annoyed.

The effort of carrying everything up here for him, along with the added physical burden of my growing womb, seemed unappreciated and unwelcomed. He could be such a jerk at times. I gently put our child and the food down in the soft green grass covered by the shade of the ash tree we had been standing under near the barrier. Walking out from under the tree boughs, hands resting on the back of my hips, I stretched my back out and yelled, "Cian!"

Everything that came next happened so fast, yet I still feel as though I am stuck in the moment. Like it is frozen in time, and I am trapped underneath it, drowning. Unable to break through the icy layer above me. Unable to reach the surface and breathe.

"CIAN!" I yelled again, waving both hands above my head this time.

My face begins to burn red hot like it's being held to fire as a few of the other men working stand up to look at me and then back over to him. I swear I can hear them laughing, further fanning the flames on my cheeks. A cloud emerges from the wounded earth where my husband's rake struck when he dropped it. Turning around, he finally acknowledged my call.

Placing his hands on his hips, he looked up to the sky before turning around to face me with the same furrowed brow from before. But his lips had changed. Dropping from a hard line into a punishing scowl, pushing the fire from my face to the rest of my body.

Dropping my arms down, I wrapped them tightly around my chest as I looked down at the ruined earth a few steps away. Clutching my dress with sweaty hands, I closed my eyes and told myself to breathe. Swallowing the lump building in my throat, I opened my eyes again to see his face, but it was changing from annoyance and anger to panic and fear. Everything changed in that moment. Time worked against me as everything moved faster than a rip current but me. I was stuck, watching helplessly for a moment as my husband screamed.

"Cael!" he yelled.

My stomach dropped and a piercing pain started in my heart. Turning around to my son and the basket I found that only the basket remained. In the few seconds it took for me to get Cian's attention, our son had already run onto the barren strip of ruined earth.

"Cael, stop!" He roared again.

Only a mischievous giggle answered. I knew the moment I saw my husband's face change, before he even uttered the first scream, that something was horribly wrong. My son's name on his lips was a deafening alarm, alerting me that my son was in danger. I turned back around as my heart beat harder, despite the protest from the sharp pains intensifying in my chest.

I heard my son's infectious giggle as I spotted his yellow shirt amongst the dark green ground foliage by the wood line. I could see his face peeking out with a mischievous, come get me smile. How could he have gotten over the ground wall? Why didn't I hear him moving past me?

"Cael!" he called, stopping a few feet short of where my son had crossed, reaching his hand out.

Six hundred seventy-nine steps. How many steps had my husband taken when he stopped short of getting our son? I'll have to ask him when the time comes. When I get back. I will get back.

Two tiny steps, backing further into the foliage. That was our son's response to my husband's calls. He was still within reach though, just an arm's reach away if my husband would only take a few steps more towards the wood line and grab him. But he didn't. He just stopped. Falling to his knees, arms now limp beside his body.

"Cael," he pleaded.

Raising one limp arm out towards our son he said, "Cael, come back to Da."

His voice broke unusually as he said, "Come on back, son."

That would be the last time he spoke to our son. The last time he said our son's name.

I didn't understand then. I still don't. Why wasn't he grabbing him? Why didn't he? He was right there. Our boy, our first born, was right there. My son looked at him, and then me with his beautiful smile. Then he turned and pointed to the woods, babbling something I could not make out before walking in.

Eight hundred and nine steps. How many steps until he was gone forever? Less than the steps I've taken so far from my hut. Less than the remaining steps to go. I can do this. I am strong enough now. Stronger than I was back then. I won't hesitate again.

I don't know why it took me so long to find my ability to move again. Why I had stayed to the side as a spectator, watching the horror unfold of my husband's inaction. But when he disappeared into the wood line I unfroze. My blood started flowing again, coursing through my veins much faster than it ever had before. I ran faster than I thought was possible, screaming his name as I did so.

"Cael!"

The acrid taste of salt and ruined earth filled my mouth after I tripped and fell over the ground level change into the barrier. I landed on my stomach and a jolt shot through me. I scrambled back to my feet, placing one hand on my belly and reaching my other hand out in the direction of my son.

"CAEL!"

I was not my husband. I was not his people. I was not afraid of the wood or what laid beyond the barrier of ruined earth. Nothing would stop me from getting my son. Not fear, not cowardice.

Finally, I was there. Right there at the edge of the wood side. Past where my husband had stopped short. Just one more step.

"Cael," I crooned softly, trying not to scare him further into the woods.

"Cael, Mama is..."

Rough hands grabbed my arms and chest, interrupting me mid-sentence and pulling me back and down with such force that it knocked the wind out of me. I looked at them as I recovered my breath.

I was confused at first. Daithí? Dolan? These were men from the village who were working the barrier today. Daithí's face was strained. Dolan's eyes wouldn't meet mine. Fear once again began to take over.

"No, no..." I took a deep breath. "NOOO!"

Desperate and angry, I fought to be free. Soon their hands were joined with those of the man in the wooden stand, the one who always stood watching the men as they worked.

"CAEL!" I yelled so hard my throat and lungs began to sting.

Only a giggle was heard in return. One that sounded much further away than it should have. Why weren't they letting me cross? Why was my husband just kneeling there, doing nothing? Why was he giving up on getting our son? My head raced with these questions. Questions that I still do not entirely have the answers to.

I fought the men holding me back harder, thrashing about like a fish caught in a net, and just as desperate. No one was going to stop me. I was going to fight them until the very end with everything I had in me.

"He's gone, Miss. You can't come back from that side once you cross," said the man from the red-stained wooden stand that stood tall on the village side bank of the barrier.

"No!" I yelled.

"Isn't it your job to ensure that no one crossed?" Daithí's voice boomed in my ear.

"I watch the woods, not the village," the man replied.

I cried as my heart fell to pieces and a hole was created inside me.

One thousand one hundred twelve steps. I was just one more step away from reaching the barrier that day. From reaching my baby. I was weak then. I couldn't fight the men who were holding me; couldn't fight through to the barrier. But I am stronger now. My skin tries to tell me I'm not, but I am. I've made it one thousand one hundred twenty-three steps now. I will not let my legs give out as they did then. I am getting close to Daithí's house. Daithí, who continued to hold me in his strong arms that day, kneeling on the ground behind me, not letting me fall alone.

"Breathe, lass," he had said, pulling my soft body into his hard chest and arms to support me. Petting my head while telling me to, "breathe."

That was the first time I surrendered to his embrace. The first time I laid my head on his shoulder and sobbed.

One thousand three hundred twenty-seven steps away from my husband.

"Cael?" I had asked him when I awoke and found myself back home in our bed.

"We will speak no more of him," he said.

He placed his hand on my growing belly, not meeting my eyes.

"*Try not to lose this one too.*"

One thousand five hundred twenty-seven steps. Only a few more until I reach Daithí's door. But the words, they echo in my mind and the weakness returns. *Try not to lose this one too.* The words are deafening, and I feel hollow again. My life. My real, true life is a nightmare. My skin in my hands. It is buzzing, telling me it can end the nightmare on land. That I can return to the Sea. I couldn't save him, what makes me think that I can save them? What makes me think Daithí will be willing to help me after I rejected him so coldly, without explanation? What makes me think he will help once I tell him the truth? Once he sees the coat in my hands? Sees that I have been here of my own will? Not captured, not forced, fighting against my own release.

One thousand six hundred thirty steps, but how many to the Sea, should I give in?

One thousand six hundred forty-eight steps. No more, no less. But I cannot bring myself to knock. I just stand there, my coat in my hands. This is it. There is no turning back. My fingers twitch, moving towards an opening in my coat, arguing that I still could return to the Sea.

"Daithí?" I begin to call weakly.

The door swings open,

"Ionna?!"

His once-young face now looks weathered. It contorts with emotion, like he can feel the intensity of my pain. Just like he did at the barrier that day, like he understood. Like he understands now.

"Daithí?" I say again before collapsing into his strong arms, which once again catch me, not letting me fall.

I wake up with my head pounding. Another nightmare? I look up and am disoriented. The room, the bed, they're not mine. The smell is lightly salty. The face I see this time is not hard and cold, it's warm like the sun. The warmth is Daithí.

This time had been longer than the others. I had managed to not go crawling back, to win him back. Now I carry the very thing that had been at the center of our last argument while it fights me the entire way.

The voice in my head continues to rail against me. I may not have been able to save Cael. I didn't fight hard enough. But I will save them. There are no hands to stop me this time. I don't need my husband. Once I get the needle, I will have everything I need. Nothing will stop me. This is pain, yes, but I have been through worse. I couldn't save him, but that's not to say it's too late. I must push forward. I must ignore the call of my own skin. It is not as strong as the call of my own blood and heart. I will make it; I will complete these jackets. Then I will go back to the barrier, and I will find my son.

"My coat?!" I stand up too quickly and the room starts to spin as I collapse back down onto the soft bed.

"It's here, it's safe. You know I would never withhold it from you, not like him." He says, spitting at the ground and running a hand through his dark wavy hair.

"When I saw you at my door, you looked like death, twisted in agony holding it so with white knuckles. All the blood seemed drained from you. You collapsed at my door and so I put it up until you were recovered." His face moving from anger at my husband to concern for me.

My body lurches forward involuntarily and I frantically look around for my coat.

"I can get it now if you want?" he says, standing up, his movements as agile and fluid as a seal underwater.

Eyes wide and wild I continue to look around as every inch of my body screams in desperation to be reunited with my coat. Daithí's hand firmly grasps my wrist, pulling me towards him gently. A warm, soothing pull in my heart moves me from the chaos and urgency of the need for my coat back to the ground where Daithí is.

"Ionna, what is going on?" Daithí asks with a tender firmness in his touch and voice.

"How are you here, with this? I didn't think it was possible for a Selkie—"

"I, uh, I need a needle," I say, turning to him and returning his touch with a much tighter grip. "Please, I need your help."

"You know, I've dreamed of you coming to me, to my door. Asking for me. A million times I've imagined this, Ionna. But I never envisioned it would be like this. You look like you've been dragged through it. Tell me what is going on? Why are you back here? How are you back here?!"

He points to the bundle of leather on his table, his one hand still holding my arm. My eyes follow his finger to where my coat lay. Suddenly I am fighting once again as every inch of my body tries to force me into launching forward to grab it, like a great shark shooting up from the depths to grab a meal.

No, I push the urge deep down inside of me. I made it. I did it. I will not answer its call now, not when I have made it this far. I keep pushing the feeling, the longing, down inside of me into a black cavern, where it continues to peek out but cannot escape.

I take a deep breath and allow my confession to flow out of me. Each word falls out one after the other, like stones spilling out from a cliff as it collapses. All the guilt and shame and worry that has been piling up inside me cascades down with my words. I no longer have the ability or time to care what he thinks, I have to save my children. I must save our child.

I need his help, needle, and knowledge to save her and her brothers. After all, he was the only one who promised to go back and look for my son at the barrier. The only one who tried to save him too. When I am finished, he lets go of my arm and sits on his bed, quietly. Looking at me with a face I cannot read. I can no longer take the silence after all I've been through to get here, I am too exhausted to linger in any more uncertainty.

"Daithí?" I start to say, but I am silenced as he stands up from the bed and turns his back to me, walking away towards the burning hearth.

I hold my breath. Maybe I was wrong? Maybe he won't help me. Maybe the revelation about my coat and the truth that I had withheld from him was too much. Panic and fear begin to bubble from deep within me, but it stops abruptly with the touch of a cold hard object in my palm, covered with the warmth of his strong, rough hand. Daithí kneels in front of me, looking up with the face I had never stopped loving, despite its absence. Unable to control myself, I shoot forward, entangling my fingers in the dark hair on the back of his head and pulling him forward until our lips meet. When I am finally able to pull myself away from his lips, I look down to see that what he pressed in my hand is a small, polished whalebone needle.

"It was my grandmother's," he says, still recovering from the assault of my lips on his.

"She taught me to sew, and a great many things. I am not very good, myself, but I will teach you, now, quickly."

I am overwhelmed. My fears about the revelations unrealized.

"Daithí," I start to say again, tears welling in my eyes.

"Shh," he says, cupping my face with his palm as my tears spill over, our lips meeting once again.

"I have and will always love you. Nothing can change that. We all have our things, Ionna. I am sorry you ever felt like you couldn't tell me something, like you had to hide something from me. It's a testament to my failure for not picking up on it, and for not proving to you that you didn't have to feel that way."

I gently wipe the tears now brimming in his own, beautiful dark eyes as they spill down his face.

He kisses me with that last word with his hand hold-ing mine to raise me up with him. I let him pull me up and turn into him. The fire between us burns out of control. The needle drops along with our bodies as we move closer into each other. Time stands still as our two bodies melt into one, the softness of my body around the firmness of his. Hands and lips urgently seek and find each other, making up for the time we have lost over the past few years.

This moment feels like a reward from the universe, giving me one last moment of sanctuary with him. One last bed of crumpled clothing to lay on. One last desperate need fulfilled. One last time of making the world wait a little longer for what it asks of me.

Ionna

The Village

8

THE WEIGHT OF HIS BLOOD

We lie here enveloped by each other's arms, fingers entwined, united in one strong fist. My head lies against the damp chest of his body as it cools off from the only fire I would ever gladly let consume me. I could never ask for anything more than this moment with him.

My head rises and falls with his chest as he breathes. His heart beats in my ear, and I close my eyes and focus on its strength. A secret nest of sea grass or the old knotty wood floor of his cottage, there isn't a place on this island where I would not open to take all of him in. I lightly graze my nails up and down his bent leg, matching the strokes of the fingertips of his free hand against my arm.

I wish I could erase everything with my husband. That I had chosen Daithí to come ashore for. That he had been the father of all my children, not just Naia. Or better yet, that we could have met in the Sea.

Sitting up and placing my hands around my knees, I see my coat laying a few feet from us, where I had dropped it to free myself for his embrace. My skin raises and tiny bumps appear. I grab Daithí's hand once more and squeeze tightly, pushing away the coat's call.

I wonder if a coat could have been made for him. I turn back to look at his face. His strong jaw is tight as he stares intently at the ceiling. I wonder if the salt in his blood would be enough, if such a thing could happen.

"The last time I saw you," he breaks our silence and my musing with a husky voice.

"I asked you to run away, and you left me. Now something is coming, and you need my help to save the children."

"I know," I say, "I'm sorry but—"

"Just listen to what I'm going to say, and don't abandon me again," he says, landing a well-deserved blow to my heart.

"I have always felt trapped here, Ionna. In this village, forced to live in a place that has never felt like home, same as you."

"Daithí, I trapped myself. It's not the same."

"That's right, because you are a Selkie and could return if it weren't for your children. But what if you didn't need to sacrifice your skin? What if you could stay with them? Stay with me?"

"What are you talking about?"

"Ionna, I've been as far out into the water as I could go, entering the mist. I got lost in it once. My boat overturned, and I was lost swimming in the water. I thought I would drown. A seal saved me, though. It pushed me to keep swimming. To push through my fear and exhaustion as it led me back to shore. What if your family led us through? Us and the children?"

"Cian would never let me take the children."

"That's not stopping you now, from making them coats from your own skin and sending them into the sea without you?"

I pull my hand back and once again wrap my arms tightly around my knees, shaking my head.

"It wouldn't work."

"Why?! Why couldn't it work? It has as much of a chance of working as cutting up your coat does. Probably even more so for the boys."

"Just stop." I stand up and grab my coat from the floor, sending painful shocks through my body as I do, like being stung by jellyfish.

"Why won't you leave with me?! Why do you keep choosing someone who doesn't love you, who doesn't see you as I have loved and seen you!?"

"I am *not* choosing Cian over you. I am choosing my children. *All* of my children over everyone, even myself. Even over what my heart desires most, which is you, Daithí."

"He's not there, Ionna. I've gone and I've looked. He's gone. For the sake of the other children, for the sake of us, you need to let go. Going into the woods will not bring him back."

"Don't say that to me. I will find him."

"You will find nothing but the misery you hold closer to your heart than anything or anyone else."

I find my way to the door through blurry, aching eyes.

"He's not there. He's not. I would have brought him back to you if he was."

I put my hand on the door, shaking.

"I am here. Caden, Aidan, Naia, we are all here. We can leave together."

I run back over to him and give him one last kiss with all the power within me.

"I love you Daithí, but I will not give up on Cael. Only Selkies can cross the mist. I'm sorry, but your blood is only enough in my heart and my dreams. I wish it were different. You do not carry the same weight in your blood as my children, as our daughter. I can and I will save them, but I am sorry that I can't save you. I have told you what is coming so that you might save yourself and others if you choose."

"I survive them by being quiet. To disrupt their peace would only serve to end me, and the outcome of what is coming would be the same, regardless," he says. I can feel the sadness coming from his beautiful dark eyes, pleading with me to stay.

"I need to go. I need to make these coats. I'm sorry. I love you, but I am sorry," I say before leaving him once again.

Ionna

The Village

9

WHAT WE HOLD IN OUR HANDS

It still feels unnatural after all these years. The five splits of my hands and their ability to move independently while still being connected at their roots in my palm. How when one is injured, it radiates through the palm where they are all connected, but the other fingers on my hand don't feel anything; they don't share the pain. Their movement will sometimes cause injury to an already injured finger. They are unaffected, and if I do not focus, they will continue to bump and move in ways that will cause pain.

I yearn for them to once again be all connected. Sometimes I think they enjoy the freedom of their independence, and who can blame them. We all at one point or another yearn to be separated from what we are so closely connected to, like young children growing braver and venturing further away from the safety of their care givers.

My coat is dried out, and after all these years, the beautiful darkness of its color has dulled and faded. The deep creases from its time spent folded refuse to smooth out, even as it lays open and splayed on the rough wooden table. I run my hands over it again and again, but the deep fold lines remain. I reach into the apron of my dress and pull out the whalebone knife. It's cool and smooth to the touch. Its color is bright white against the dull shades of brown and grey around me.

I miss the way my skin looked before I came on land, dark and beautiful. How the water would roll off of it, making it shimmer in the sun. I wonder if my skin will regain its beauty once it becomes my children's; if they can revive it with their youth and freedom once they're in the water. If they can even transform. If the Sea will even take them.

The dryness of my coat is met with the roughness and dampness of my palm as I push down upon it with one hand and bring the bone knife in my other to meet my skin. Three coats, three different sizes. I place the shaking knife point down and press it into my skin. Tiny droplets of the first salt water my coat has touched in years begins to fall upon my skin. The tears leave tiny dark spots that my coat quickly absorbs. I take a deep breath in and as I slowly blow it out, the warmth of a skinny arm wraps around my waist. A warm, calloused hand covers the top of mine that is holding the knife.

"It's okay, Momma," Caden's voice says softly from where his head lies on my shoulder.

"I know you can do this. It's okay if it's not like the ones the mothers in the village do."

My breath catches. Deep down he is still my sweet boy. He has no idea how right he is. These coats will not be like the ones from the village.

He is the most like my husband, the most like the villagers. I will give him the biggest piece of me because he needs it the most. Naia and Aidan, they embrace the Sea and their Sea family. With his hand on mine, we make the first long cut together. I know he can't feel my pain as we drag the knife down my skin.

He may move independently and away from me by his father's side, but he and his brothers and sister are still connected at their roots to me and to the Sea. He is still my baby, and of the Sea. I will make his first, and then Aidan's. I will make sure the Sea will give them the same chance it will give their sister, despite their lesser Selkie blood.

Ionna

The Village

10

TINY FROWNS IN THE DARKNESS

"Damn." The intense pain of the sharp, bleached white bone needle piercing my fingertip screams at me to stop. It's the fourth time tonight after the countless times I had stuck myself today since making the initial cut with Caden. Tiny droplets of dark red blood and silent tears now adorn the last of the small, crude jackets I am rushing to finish. The pain in my head and fingers grow, contrasting with the waning fire and its dimming light from our hearth. Vague shadowy figures born of the glowing embers dance around me, mocking me as they weave in and out, clouding my vision at times. The uneven lines of stitching and bunching on the dark grey leather look like a line of tiny frowns in the darkness.

The warmth of the dying fire itself calls to me like a lost lover. It beckons me to rest in the comfort of its arms, which stretch out of the hearth seductively.

My heavy eyes are begging me to answer the call as I struggle to ignore them.

I want to close my eyes and forget about everything that my sisters warn is coming in their songs. Forget about my conversation with Aine on the beach that morning. Forget about the sadness and emptiness that has followed me all these years. Forget about the war between hope and hopelessness that has been raging inside my soul. About what is lost, and what may be lost yet. My will is hanging on by this very thread that I continue to push and pull through the leather. I know that if I give up on my task and surrender to the fire's call, I will fail. There are no other options before me... and even less time.

I put my throbbing fingertip in my mouth and try to focus on easing the pain. The taste of my blood is salty, like the water below our hut that my heart has ached for since I left. My family sleeps peacefully and soundly in the old, worn bed, covered in tattered blankets that once matched the illusion of joy and promise that comes with newness. Blankets that should be whole. If I were a wife like the other women in the village, they would be.

The loft above us is empty, as three of our children crowd my husband as they sleep. Sweet faces still glow from the warmth of yesterday's afternoon sun. Freckles line the bridges of my sons' noses. My daughter's skin is the only one untouched by the marks of the sun's warm kisses. My husband seems unaware or unbothered by their encroachment.

I find a space in the bed with them where Cael should be. Even though it looks like there isn't anything missing in a family, like there isn't any more room in a bed, I can always see an outline of where my son should be. The outline of what is missing, of what makes our life and our family not full. The outline of the anchor that keeps me tethered to this land. To that moment that I am always reminded of, telling me I am the reason my son is not, that we are not.

You couldn't save him, what makes you think you can save them? That intrusive voice breaks through the wall I had just put up.

I have already overcome so much to get what I needed to make these jackets. The small victories don't mean anything when the task is not yet complete, though. "You couldn't save him," becomes "You can't save them," making my stomach drop and my throat tighten. That voice continues to grow louder and louder as each day passes since Aine's warning, continuing to interrupt my thoughts and progress. It increases the sense of loneliness that haunts me during these late-night hours. My body aches with need for Daithí's touch again after leaving him this morning.

Clenching the needle and jacket in one hand and the edge of our splintered wooden table with the other, I try to steady myself. My heartbeat starts throbbing in my ears, and the room begins to spin as the pain in my finger fades to the background. The dancing shadows and darkness where the light from the fire doesn't reach combine. Tightening my grip, I suck in a sharp breath as the needle jabs painfully into my hand. The pain from where it enters my palm brings me back, and my focus slowly returns.

I release my grip and see another dark red bead appearing. Another adornment for my children's coats. I focus on the small pool of blood forming in my palm, and the pain from the needle. Breathe. Breathe. Breathe. I force myself to push past the searing pain of the past and the crippling panic of the future.

Breathe. This time the voice is not my own, but of the old woman from the village. The only one brave enough to help a strange woman give birth to what they all believed would be a strange child.

"Remember to breathe," she had instructed me when the pain in my back and bottom became too intense for me to do anything but cry. Normally a birth was an event that multiple women from the village would attend, but not mine. They saved their curiosity of whether our child would have webbed feet or devil's horns for the streets I dread walking, that I avoid walk-

ing. Back then, I thought there was no greater pain than that of childbirth, and no greater sadness and sense of loneliness than that of being separated from the sea. Even if voluntarily so.

"I can't do this!" I cried out to the old woman as the pain peaked, and I felt as though I would completely fall apart.

"They all say that," she replied, then ordered me to push.

Soon my son was there, and I was filled with a sense of relief and joy. The old woman cleaned him off and gave him to me before making her way to the door.

"Wait!" I called out. "Don't leave yet. Please. I don't know what to do."

With a soft smile she said, "Just listen to your body. Your natural instinct as a mother will guide you."

I wanted to tell her that nothing about giving birth in this form felt natural to me. The reality of being a mother away from the Sea, away from my family, finally hit me and increased the sense of loneliness. Even with the promise of happiness and sense of love and purpose that came from my newborn son, the feeling of being alone, of being detached and vulnerable, made me feel like I was drowning in that moment, and continued for many months after. I wanted my sisters. I wanted the Sea. I wanted us to be surrounded by the encouraging sound of the waves lapping at the rocks around a whelping bed.

"Please," I said again.

"You need to learn to do this on your own."

"Why, why did you come to help me at all?!"

"I could never stand to see the sight of a wounded animal."

She walked out the door and I held my baby close to my heart as we both cried. She was right, partly. But I was not totally alone. My son and I, we figured it out together those first few months. He taught me how to be a mother. His siblings have him to thank for teaching me how to care for them. Through his tears in that first year as we both learned, theirs would be lessened. I wish he was still here, still teaching me. That we were still learning together.

The old woman continued to return for each of my children's births, and she continued to leave right after they took their first breaths, except for my daughter. When she caught my last baby in her old, knowing hands, she just held her, staring at her with big eyes framed by the marks of time and experience. Both silent.

"What's wrong?!" I asked.

But the old woman did not answer. She continued to gaze upon my child in silence.

"Bring her to me!" I demanded, panic rising in me.

My youngest son Aidan, who had been holding my hand, echoed my request, "Bring baby, Mama, now!"

He had insisted on staying home with me to make sure I was okay. Though he favored his father in looks, like his older brother Caden, he was always very attached and in tune with me. His presence always helped me to calm down in moments of stress. He was excited to welcome what he declared was "his baby."

It's funny, the way siblings can be so alike and so different in many ways. Caden reminded me of our first born, Cael, in some ways. They have the same sweetness and laugh. Caden was so different from my younger children though. He gravitated towards his father and his people, always eager to go with him to the fields or helping with the fishing nets instead of staying home with us. From a young age, whenever given the chance he would always insist on accompanying his father to the village or to work.

"Nothing is wrong, big brother," she said, answering my Aidan's demand after her long silence. She chuckled while she finished cleaning off and wrapping my daughter up in linen the color of pale sunshine—the only gift I would receive from a villager for any of my children's births after the loss of Cael.

"Here you go, Mother," she said, handing my baby girl to me.

That was the only time the old woman stayed. Sitting on the edge of my bed, she stroked my daughter's head, which was already covered in thick, dark curly hair, *with her old knowing hands. That was the only time I didn't feel alone giving birth.*

I have spent so much time thinking about each of my children's births lately. So much time thinking about the past and path that have led me here these last few nights. About that old woman. About her words to me about learning to do this on my own. About being a wounded animal. She was right about everything. I am a wounded animal. But wounded animals, we can be dangerous, unpredictable. Our strength, despite our pain, is often underestimated, especially when cornered. I know something is coming this time, and I will do more this time to save my children.

The throbbing in my palm brings me back from the memory. I look at the needle, no longer bleach white, but stained with my blood. My resolve grows stronger.

"You need to learn to do this on your own," the old woman had said.

But she was only partly right. In the needle, I am reminded I have Daithí, and in my blood, my sisters and the Sea. One tiny, dark grey jacket left to finish. Just three pieces left to sew together. I sit back down, determined to stay awake and finish Naia's coat. I saved hers, the smallest of the three, for last. She has the most salt in her blood. She needs the least amount of my skin. The cuts I made for her coat have been the easiest. I hum quietly to calm my nerves and drown out the relentless, intrusive voice in my head as I resume my work. My husband doesn't like it when I hum, but he's asleep and shouldn't be bothered by it. It's an old song, of the devil in the sea, the devil on the land, and the one who captured me.

Ionna

The Village

11

THEY'RE HERE

I am almost done; I can almost catch a little breath.

Though my husband has dismissed my warnings and worries from the warning sirens from the Sea, I think deep down he must know something is coming. I believe that is why he has not said another word about me cutting up my coat, or where the needle and my newly found sewing skills have come from. Nothing crosses the mist, my husband says.

A coat from a coat has never worked before, other than the old story of the Selkie maid. Selkie coats are meant for our skin only. Non-Selkies have tried to wear them before, failing attempts to transform or using them as charms to trick the Sea into granting calm waters or bountiful catches. To anyone but us, it's the same as any other animal hide.

Our children are half of the Sea. I do not know the words to sing, but I pray to Mother Sea that these coats, my blood, and prayer in song will be enough to grant them safe passage home. That she will accept them. Should it work, it should also grant them the ability to cross the mist with the rest of the colony.

Aine has talked about the potential need to migrate, should her fears of what's to come be realized. Grant them another option to leave, to escape, to move on. I begin to sew another line of tiny frowns that will join the final piece, the last little sleeve in place. I take another pause to look over at my husband's face before I continue working the needle and thread in and out of the soft leather. It has become softer as I have worked on it throughout the day and night. I wish I was still looking upon Daithí's face instead of my husband's.

I allow myself a brief smile at the image of him wrapped up with me on the floor after our last meeting. After we leaned into the inescapable need for our bodies to connect, before I had to leave him once more. Now I know the only thing I can ever truly love more than the Sea is my children.

After that walk to his house, and the feeling that still lingers from our embrace, I think I could also love Daithí more. I wonder if he would come with me to the barrier when this is over. I wonder if that is something I can even ask after refusing his request to escape together into the mist. I think he would come; I know he does not hold the same fear of it as the other villagers. He was the only one who went back for my son. The only one who crossed the barrier to look for and bring him back if he found him.

Bark! Bark!

My heart stops at the urgent barking coming from the beach down below our hut.

It's different than the plaintive warnings they had been singing. No longer a song, but an urgent command to get out now. Fear rises from my stomach, freezing my blood before my heart suddenly starts pounding again, this time with violence. There is no more time to reflect on the past. Their barking brings all my attention to the present. It awakens my husband, whose eyes fly open while keeping his body soft and still to not disturbed the children, who are somehow still sleeping, unbothered by the shrill barks.

"Ionna?" he asks in a quiet, alarmed voice.

"They're here," I say, each word beating its way out of my throat and mouth.

EINAR

THE WOODSIDE BEACH

12

GIRL WITH THE GLOW

I remember the weight of Father's hand as it laid heavily on my shoulder. "Tools were made to serve, Einar." His fingers curled over my shoulder, applying more pressure. "Not to love."

Peeling my gaze off the girl with the glow, I said, "Yes, Father."

I would spend much of my time getting caught stealing glances at her until I finally became more proficient at controlling myself. It seemed like a reward, that after I finally learned control and restraint she would walk into my room to undo it. Slowly, intentionally extinguishing all the light in my room until the only one left was her. Bare skin moved gracefully. Snuffing one candle at a time with her long, delicate fingers, she had never glowed so brilliantly as she did there in the darkness of my room. A stark contrast to the broken thing that lay before me now.

Her skin now glistens from the cold sweat that comes before death, transforming it to something so foreign from the beauty she had been. Her long, golden hair no longer glows, despite the enclosing darkness of the evening. So far from the clear vision burned into my memory of her in full glory the first night I held her in my arms, her long hair spilling over my trembling hands during our first touch. Flowing over and in between my fingers like a river of honey. The taste of her filling a desperate craving that had been building since I first laid eyes on her.

I can still hear the echoes of Father's deep voice in my ear as I look where she lay crumpled on the ships deck.

"A leader is only as good as his control."

Father did not face me as we looked into the training pits where the newest acquisition of boys—warriors—were being lined up. Most were my age. Some looked younger.

"Father." I stepped forward, but dared not touch him, though I wanted to grab his hand and make him look at me. "They're so young?"

"Control over people, Einar. Control over themselves."

Father moved so quickly as he hoisted me into the air.

"It's time for you to learn to master this so you will be ready to lead them," he said.

I fell from the platform above the other children to the pit floor. As they stood above me, the last word I heard from Father was, "Control."

Seals barking in the distance brings me out of the memory of my father and his words, which still guide me. I suppress any sign that they startled me. I am in control, always. Control is my mantra. Control is my fervent prayer as a range of emotions caused by the quick deterioration of the girl jockey for position, each threatening to break loose and wreak havoc within me. The Hamingja looks increasingly dull, damp, and cold. Her light and life are fading slowly. First into paleness, then darkness that sneakily creeps in through her fingertips. It seeps into the rest of her body like a traitor's poison, stealthily working its way through her veins.

There was a time when I thought the only places where darkness could touch her, mask her light, were the places where she and I connected in my room. That was the only place where I could give up my control. Those were the only times.

The Hamingja's breath changes ever so slightly as Bjorn softens his hard body to gently pick her up. He was always the soft one, even as a child, never able to exhibit any sort of control over his emotions.

Though we are the same age, he carries the burdens of the years past more than I or the others. The stress caused by his lack of control age him more and more lately, and his russet fur begins to fade into a roan. I fight back the sense of worry that I am losing him. The furrow of his brow, the hard line of his lips, let me know he is ill-equipped to deal with the burdens of a long death. It's a concept too strange for him and the rest of the brothers to understand, to notice.

Their experiences have always been the short, sudden and brutal deaths. The agonizing, violent ones. It's why they did not pick up on the signs of Father's impending death, but the Hamginja and I did. It is why she came to me that night, telling me to talk my father into gifting her to me before he passed. We both saw the subtle changes signaling the unstoppable end. The change in skin, in breathing, in rational thought. I am surprised none of them could smell it on him, given their abilities. The abilities that I should have but lack. The day Father realized I was his failed experiment remains with me.

"There are men who are bears, and there are men who fight and conquer them," Father's voice came firmly from behind me as I held a bloodied washcloth to my face after my first day in the pits.

Hatred was the first emotion I learned to control. I understood his intention. I was to be the latter, like him. I was the genius of his plan to "unite", as he would say, the entire land. It was better to let him think the blood came from the pits and not from the fall when he threw me.

I still feel the weight of his hand on my shoulder when he turned me towards him as he spoke. "People need to be ruled, to be controlled. They cannot be counted on to do what is best for us, or themselves. They need people like us to guide, to control. Serving our will *is* what serves them best. You will help me make them realize this."

I still feel the pressure from him, his fingers squeezing my shoulder as he said, "My son."

Father appeared to lose sight of his will towards the end as his death progressed. It made his decisions unreliable, and we suffered great losses. His vision was cloudy, distorted, and he couldn't see. I had to do what was best for all of us, for Father. It was time to serve my will. The men will never know what I did was a mercy killing, for Father as much as for them.

Father was the man who fought and conquered the bears. He raised his only son with theirs to ensure the next generation's unwavering allegiance to him through me. I alone bear the weight of the responsibility of my father's legacy, my legacy, and the survival of our people. I alone bear the responsibility of the creation of a new world—a better world. The time of the good death is over. I alone will bring the flow of milk and honey to our people. I alone will bring the time of a good life over a good death.

The dying girl winces in Bjorn's arms, and it's clear her pain causes an involuntary wincing of his own. It won't be long for her now. I had hoped bringing her would ensure the success of our mission into the woods, but the trip through the mist seems to have proved too much for her. Her light and life are used up. Father had warned me that a Hamingja's powers were finite, to use their luck sparingly to ensure our success. I burned her candle too low, and now her light is going out.

That is the problem with using other people's luck, you can never count on it for your own success, to see you all the way through, no matter how promising it may seem. You can only ever count on your own luck. Luck that is earned. Luck that is won. Luck that is entirely your own. I have come to realize what I should have during those nights in my room: she was never my own.

As Bjorn walks past me to carry the girl to the shore, she uses what little strength she has to reach her arm out to me. The way she beckons me with her waning strength, her dying breaths, her outstretched hand reminds me of my mother. I can still see a small flicker of flame in her eyes as they look to me to take her hand. I turn my head away as Bjorn carries her past me. I feel the deathly cold fingers of her outstretched arm pleading for acknowledgment on my skin as they pass. I start to feel warmth build under my skin. No! I violently push the sensation away with my mind. I am in control. I AM.

I move towards the back of the ship, away from the shore as Bjorn continues to carry the Hamingja off. Mads follows him, as do the rest of the men. I stare out at the sea, at the wall of mist she saw us safely through. The mist that seems to have taken all that was in her.

"She was a tool," I hear Father's voice whisper firmly.

My body fights against my will to shudder at the memory of her cold touch a few minutes ago. From how different it felt from the warmth of her skin against mine back home.

"Say my name," her lips would whisper in my ear.

"Freyda," I would murmur as I drifted off to sleep, basking in her light.

BJORN

THE WOODSIDE BEACH

13

THE DEBT

Life is a debt. That was the last thing my beautiful mother said to me. Paid or owed, it's a debt either way. I didn't understand what her words meant for a long time. I was so young when she said them. I wish with all my being I didn't understand them now. As I look at the dying girl's limp body on the ground, propped against the bottom of the prow of the long-boat, I am reminded of the last time I saw my mother.

The large carved serpent head above the dying Hamingja looks menacing, and I clutch the dark stone that hangs at the bottom of the worn brown leather strap around my neck. I grip it with enough force to crush a man's skull, wishing I never had to feel this way again. Wishing I could measure in something besides violence and death.

I was young when Einar's father first sought us out to join his army. My brother, Stellan, was younger than I. There isn't much I remember about her anymore.

The memories continue to fade over the years, at times replaced by the evolving idea of my mother in my mind. I can't even tell you if the image of her in my head is true, or something I created over time. Little details change here and there as my memory becomes unreliable, like the shape of her face or the exact shade of her dark russet hair and the way she wore it. At least I think it was the same color as ours.

Stellan remembers even less. Maybe that is why he is uninterested in conjuring up lost memories. The weight of her dying gaze, the words and warning she told me before I was taken as a replacement for my father. Before my brother was taken as a spare in case my hamr was not as strong as our father's. Those memories remain intact.

Father had died in battle a week before, and a replacement for him was owed. She had died the day they came for us. She told me life is a debt, but she refused to pay my father's with us. Father's ability to change his shape in battle is what made him, and potentially us, so valuable as warriors. As those with hamrammr. She told us to hide as she left to meet the men who came at the front of our house, but I didn't listen, and Stellan followed me into disobedience as we followed her.

From around the corner in a spot we thought was hidden on the side of the house, we watched as she made her stand against them with the fierceness of a cornered animal desperate to protect its young. We watched as she fought to the last dying breath. Watched as she fell with a heavy thud. Watched as both her eyes, and the men's, fell upon the spot that was not as hidden as I had thought.

I carry with me her last look before death, and the weight of the disappointment in her eyes before they closed forever. Her final image being that of me failing her. Failing my little brother. Stellan had grabbed my hand and tried to get me to run as mother fought them. I was bigger than him, and he was stuck frozen in place as the men came towards us, tethered to me with fingers locked in fear that intertwined in an inescapable grip with his.

Our life, our childhood, died right there when she did. Our new life as warriors, one of the last lines of berserkers, began. I sometimes wonder what our life would have been like if I had listened and hid as she instructed. She would have died just the same, but we would not have been captured. Stellan would not be on his own separate journey towards sacrifice. Maybe it wouldn't have made a difference; death is what makes life possible. Death, it comes for us all. This we all know. This is the universal truth for all things. Yet still, the first death I was responsible for, the one that gave birth to the me I am now, that sealed my fate, was that of my mother.

When his father, the self-proclaimed King of All People, first took us, I was angry and scared. I knew nothing about balancing life and death. At first, I was too influenced by the anger and fear of what felt like abandonment by my parents; like a betrayal of something I was born into without choice that placed me into a life of forced servitude.

King Erik and his men gave me a place to channel that anger and sadness. I was taught how to use that emotion to generate the hamrammr I needed to change. In time, the anger and sadness were joined by the feeling of companionship, loyalty and devotion to my brothers, who had been sought out and taken as Stellan and I had. We became all we had, and the cause to unite the country became a personal one for us.

In battle, no longer caged in with iron bars, we were free to let out our anger, our sadness, and replace it with the high that came from unleashing what had begun to feel like our true forms. With each life we took, we were buying into a promise. The battlefield, the lives we took, it became an addiction, a gamble on the investment of being able to build a better future with death, or to die and be rejoined with our fallen fathers and brothers. Not just for us, but for our people, for our world. Even as we slaughter part of it, it is the cost of progress.

What I realize now is all I was doing all those years with King Erik's army, as one of his caged beasts of war, was creating a life debt for myself. A debt that now feels unpayable, unsatisfiable. I am left bearing the weight of the grief from thousands of souls lost. The weight of their cries, their spirits, is so heavy it threatens to crush me.

Once the blood lust started to wear off after years of battles and slaughter, the feeling that we were not making any progress towards unification became too strong to ignore, to rationalize. Every day, every week, felt the same. I started to lose myself on the battlefield as I had seen happen to others. Statues mid-strike, faces dripping in fresh blood, suspended in time as violence continued to rage around them. I tried to ignore it at first, that sinking feeling that comes with the realization of how much you have fucked yourself.

For me, it started the night he killed his father in the great hall of our capital. The night we stopped fighting, and realized that the promise of a unified land for all our people, for us, was never going to happen. The promise of no more fighting for scraps of barren land. No more starving for lack of food or thirsting for lack of good water.

Unification was supposed to be better, to do away with the greed and rationing of resources between territories and create a land of shared resources. It's a heavy blow to one's soul, to lose one's purpose. The realizations from that night still haunt me. The blood still pumps loudly in my ears, and the acidic taste rises in my throat every time the memory comes back to me.

All those people, all those lives. Not a paid debt, but a debt owed. A debt I have no way of paying back unless Einar's plan works. Einar killed his father that night before we could council, discuss or act. He stepped in and did what needed to be done.

I think he knew we all just had the vision of what we had been fighting for since we were children smashed in front of us. Even though we were raised as brothers and treated the same in his father's army, he felt responsible for our fate. As if all those years had been his own doing. As if he hadn't been right there next to us in the pits, on the battlefield. He sacrificed his love for his father for us. He did what had to be done and gave us a hope, a path forward to mend the vision we had been sold on and execute it in a better way. One that accrued less debt. One that gave a small glimmer of hope that maybe we could repay what we had spent under his father's false pretenses.

Einar was always a good man, a good leader. He spoke his words carefully, with intention. He listened to and respected every viewpoint, even encouraging opposing views, wanting to hear and learn from both sides. He was so unlike his father in that way. We were not just beasts of violent burden to him; we were his brothers. When it was your turn to speak to him, he had a way of making you feel like everything you said was important and mattered, even if he disagreed with you.

I always thought I would follow him blindly to the end of the earth and into the great hall at our deaths, but that night I had my first meeting with doubt and regret. When faced with the realization that the unification would never happen and what was now owed from the debt of a failed campaign, I was ready to take my life. I saw no other way out, and I couldn't take the overwhelming sense of hopelessness, guilt and shame. I couldn't take the looks from the thousands of eyes I gave over to death laying upon me. The death eyes of my mother, that I can still feel watching my every move in disappointment.

Einar never let the weight of other eyes affect him. He walked right in and took his father's life so easily, so matter of fact, as if no one was watching. We were but 20 then, his father still in the last years of his prime, and Einar did it with such grace that his father crumpled in awe.

Some say he had a smile on his face as his heart slowly stopped pumping the blood out from his body. I wouldn't know. I couldn't look. I couldn't stand another vision of a parent laying their eyes on the child who was causing them to shut forever.

Einar apologized to us on behalf of his father, wiping the blood off his hands and blade with his father's shirt before gently closing his father's eyes. I tried to tell him the choices of our parents are not our fault, not our responsibility, and not ours to bear. He gave me a comforting smile, laid his hand upon my shoulder and thanked me, comforting me as I intended to comfort him.

He laid out a new path forward, a path towards forgiveness and independence and meaning. A path to make things right. A path we felt we had a say in. He put it to a vote to those of us who were there that night, a vote that didn't need to happen. We were with him, always with him. I thought back then that I was voting for the greater good, done correctly this time. I once again found purpose that night, found hope. I never doubted him back then.

Squeezing the little black rock in my hands again, I know now that I cannot bear the terms of repayment. I have only one life to pay with—my own. But my life is not enough. I wish I could crush this stone, this heart of darkness that I fear matches my own. That symbolizes the darkness and loneliness I believe awaits me at death if I cannot repay my debt. But it's all I have left of Stellan. He gave it to me the night we learned of his fate. The night I shamed my brother, failing him once more by going to Einar behind his back and begging him to send another.

"Brother," Stellan had said with love in his eyes. Love I did not deserve. "Take this, let it help you navigate your darkness."

He pressed the stone into my hand, kissing me on the cheek and giving me one great bear hug before leaving me alone. Mads and I had gone with him to retrieve it, to learn the way to find the heart of the sun from the old man who hid in the high caves above the falls and the sea.

There was no light in his heart, only darkness. Cutting open his chest, no light shone brightly, only this dark, hard stone—the man's dark heart. Handing it to Stellan, he warned him of what he would become if he was not worthy of the sun's love, should he even survive the journey through fire and sand to reach her before collapsing and crumbling into dust.

Nausea slowly creeps in before the eve of a battle or mission. Headaches began in the aftermath of what I have done and continue to do. Tightness in my chest comes at night when I desperately try to turn my mind off enough to sleep but can't.

Every time I say I can't do this anymore, but I must. Every time I say I never want to feel like this again, but then I do. I hold the stone, the heart of the night, and wish for Stellan to come back. I wish for all of this to end. I wish that the stone would show me a way through the darkness, but it doesn't. It just weighs against my chest, above the surface of where my own heart beats.

It reminds me of Stellan and the ways I've failed him, and the ways he has continued to love me, regardless. Maybe if I could conjure the same faith in this stone to guide and protect me that Stellan has, it would work. Stellan's mind never strays into the darkness and despair where mine seems to dwell.

Looking down at the weak figure leaning against the prow of the longboat, I release the stone from my hand. I can feel the blood in my head start to pound against my ears, and the nausea slowly begins. The bright illumination of her skin that was so noticeable in the beginning, that shone almost as bright as the light of an evening star, is unnoticeable now. Her skin is now overcast with the dense cloud and fog that had made her star's light illumination disappear. The only hint of any light left in her is a hint of smokey grey that still flickers in her eyes, dancing like a small flame not yet extinguished in the embers of a fire close to death. It took everything in her to see us safely through the mist of Hel and onto this island. She is soon another life taken, another debt owed. All the nerve endings in my skin come alive, and the left side of my chest begins to ache. A prayer, a demand, a desperate plea repeats over and over inside me to make this feeling stop.

"Great, we are finally arriving, and the Hamingja decides to leave." says Mads, who comes to stand beside me. His brightly colored ornate tunic contrasts with the darkness of my mood, the night, and our present situation.

"Next time bend down so she can hear you a little better."

"Always so grumpy these days, Bjorn. I doubt she is strong enough to comprehend what's going on around her at this point. Or care much if she does in her current state." He continues as he waves his hand dismissively at the girl. "Look at her, she knows she's dying. I'll not feel bad for speaking such an obvious truth, the girl is not dumb."

Mads crosses his arms so matter of fact. His ability to remain smug and bubbly no matter the situation or location has always irritated me. At the same time, it also has a way of releasing some of the tension, which I always appreciate.

I look down at her with a serious face, my eyes straining from the growing pain in my head.

"If she does care, it won't be for much longer. Look at her. She is done, Brother. And so may we be, too, if he can't get what he brought us here for. If we can't get back out through that Hel mist."

"Fucking Choking Mist," Mads says, spitting on the ground by our feet.

Though Mads always puts on a face of bravery and humor, I can tell the journey through the mist has unnerved him, as it has to us all. Except maybe Einar.

"Trying to drown out my colors," Mads laughs, shaking off the fleeting show of nerves as he punches my shoulder from a hand's length away.

I resist the urge to rub my shoulder where he hit me or give him the satisfaction of acknowledging that it hurt.

"I know how much you guys like them," he says, a smug smile and playful glint in his eyes.

As much as I want him to be wrong about the girl, I know what he says is true. She is too weak to stand, to be saved. If she does survive our time on the island, she will not survive the trip back through the fog and sea. Her usefulness is spent, and I don't foresee there being any extra energy or resources available to spend on something without use.

Mads and I continue to survey the girl and form a barrier between her and the others who may have other ideas about her usefulness. I feel a subtle, calming change in the air, and I know Einar is near. His presence commands love, respect and awe. Despite knowing him from childhood, I still am not immune to the presence he commands. It's why after all these years he can still successfully command me. He needs me, and I need to help him be successful if I can. It's the only thing that matters, no matter what it ends up costing me. His success is my redemption.

Mads and I part to make room for Einar between us, each taking a step back as well so as not to crowd him. To see him is to be taken back by the charm he exudes. Though he is not as large as Mads and I physically, standing a full foot shorter, or as broad, he has a way of carrying himself which makes him seem like the largest, strongest person in the room. His dark hair hangs neatly to his shoulders, always plaited. He looks down at the girl, his face perfectly calm.

"Child, you've done good," his voice matches his face. "But the night is not over; your task is not yet complete."

He remains standing as he surveys the girl, looking upon her broken body. He must see that what little she has left in her will be of no use to us. The girl manages to look up at him from where she lies crumpled on the ground, the strain evident on her glistening face. They say at the end, everything becomes clear to you. You can see through all the bullshit of your life and see what was real and what was not. Despite the dimness, there is still a small spark in her eyes, and I believe she can see. Her face, which had shown with such love, such devotion in the beginning of our journey, is now bitter and cold as she uses what little strength she can muster to speak.

"I have served my purpose thus far, yet it's still not enough." The girl understands her new position. In her final moments, she seems not to care about Einar's.

"You have used everything. There is nothing left." Each word of her reply seems to take a great deal of effort. She sinks a little further into the ship she is leaning against.

"Shame," Einar says in a tone layered in disappointment and disapproval which would break the hearts of any of these big, strong men, including myself. Yet the girl is strangely immune now, using whatever remaining strength she has to lash out at Einar as he turns away from her.

"May you face the inevitable death that awaits you on this island, in that dark wood, in the same calm, cruel manner in which you have used me!" Her voice rises as she yells at his back. "You led me here, led these men here, to meet death that will be by your hands. By your doing."

The others who are within range begin to walk over, called by her words.

"Remember, fair, honored, respected, loved one, should you utter one hint of a scream, if one part of you is afraid in there, you will never ascend to feast in the great halls with your fathers, with your brothers."

Her words turn Einar back to face her.

"You fail to understand," he says as he steps forward and once again looks down upon her, "I didn't kill you; you have done that by your own effort and inabilities."

Crouching down to face the girl, he continues in a quiet voice I can barely hear.

"Make no mistake, no ascension waits for me. No divine to carry me up. My plans have a far greater purpose than myself, my men. And more than you. So, I say to you now, rest. You did your job as well enough as you were able." His words send shock waves through me as he stands back up, looking down at the girl once more. I struggle to make sense of his words to her. What they mean to her. What they should mean to me.

"Release the poison from your tongue and heart. It'll weigh you down and you'll be stuck in this place, or worse." He turns his back on the girl and faces us now.

"Say my name!" The girl calls out with dying breaths.

Einar ignores her and beckons for us to walk with him.

"Say my name!" She demands again, but her voice is weak. She cannot command him.

Einar stops our walk just out of earshot of the girl. Though a few years older than me, he still looks young, as if untouched by the many years and battles we have faced together. There are no visible signs of the stress of growing up in the wars of his father, or the emotional toll of patricide. He is as he's always been: unmarked, unbothered, and beautiful.

I hate him for how he's been so unscathed by all we've been through, when it's brought me to the brink of no longer being able to be present at times. I can feel the anger bubbling up in my stomach, the heat replacing the nausea caused by the shock waves. My skin prickles again, and I am in danger of losing myself and changing completely. My whole body begins to vibrate. What did he mean, no ascension waits for him? Does he fear death? No, I have seen him in battle many times, there has never been any hint of fear in him.

Einar looks past us, surveying the men on the beach behind us, the boat, and the dying girl. He reaches out and puts his hand firmly on my shoulder, letting it rest there. The weight and warmth of his hand instantly stops the vibration of my body, the anger that was starting to seep through the outer layers of it as he begins to address us. As the anger begins to retreat, a sense of calm radiates from his hand through my shoulder and straight into my heart, my skin smoothing back over like waves calming after a dark storm. I love him as much as I hate him. The passion is the same both ways.

"I need you, Bjorn." he says, and just like that, everything fades, and it is only me and him.

"I want us to be as efficient as possible, we cannot afford to make mistakes. We have no idea how long it will take, and we must succeed. I need you to help me succeed. To help us all. Mads, we need you to come in with us to assure the mission is successful. Bjorn."

I feel a slight reassuring increase in pressure from his hand as he addresses me again.

"I need you to stay here, taking care of the ship and the men is important. If something happens to the ship-"

His words fade as I once again feel the prickling sensation move across my skin. I imagine if his hand wasn't on my shoulder right now, I would be losing my shit. He knows I hate the others. I don't trust them. I don't care for them. Another reassuring slight increase in pressure brings me back, and I can hear his words once more.

"Protecting the boat is an honor. If anything happens to it, it's all over."

He emphasizes the last part to me so I will understand, and I do, but I don't like it.

"There's a village up the beach a few miles," Mads interjects, "just on the other side of those cliffs. I saw the lights after we broke through the mist. Surely the extra men you brought can watch the boat, and should something happen to it, we can raid the village for another boat, or supplies to repair."

I look at Mads as he looks at me, hands resting on his hips, his stance slightly slouched, giving off a relaxed appearance, but his eyes are a little wider than normal, betraying him. I know he shares the same concern of me not coming with them. We've had each other's backs since we were children, and I've saved him more times than we can both count. He's a good warrior, built large and strong, if not a little eccentric in his dress and humor, favoring the long tunics like those of a woman. He is surprisingly agile for his size and dress, but he gets frenzied in battle and can lose sight of his surroundings, which leaves him open to being misled during battles or missions. The last time I saw Mads this uneasy was the night we met the Volva.

Einar had taken a small group of us past the short stone border wall into the dark vast woods of the far north to meet her. The woods were known to be filled with wizards and trolls and a number of other beings. The wall was built as a warning by our ancestors, to keep us from venturing in. We were lucky we did not lose any men that night, but the things we saw and heard still haunt many of us.

She was beautiful, the Volva. Not at all old or a crone like the name "Grandmother Volva" would have suggested. Her hair flowed dark and long like a river down her back and sides. Something about her took our breath away in a frightening way, like the coldest winter air in our lungs. Her dress was a dark grey blue with tiny gems that twinkled and shone like the stars in the night sky that we were so desperate to see but couldn't through the thick forest canopy.

She whispered in Einar's ear at times with lips as red, and maybe as poisonous, as the berries found in the woods back home. She had said this island would be dangerous; especially the woods and the creatures it held within it. As if anything could be more dangerous than the woods we stood in with her at that moment. The large wooden altar she had appeared from behind seemed to emphasize her warning about the woods. The polished white bone of the largest bear skull I had ever seen planted seeds of fear and doubt in my heart. She told us to leave the village, to go into the woods and return before dawn. There was another Einar was to meet who would provide him with the knowledge for us to succeed and build the new life and nation that we all deserved and were desperate for. A place where we could finally have peace after living our entire lives in war.

She had also warned of the great cost that would come with it, but we have already spent so much. The burden of the cost has been great for so long that adding more to it for the chance to be free was something that, even while struggling to breathe from the crushing weight of the lives I've taken which continue to haunt me, seemed worth it. I would do anything for a chance to eventually be free of it.

I sometimes go back over the many battles, missions, or instances where I've taken a life in my head and see where I could have done things differently. How I could have avoided the mass grave I have and continue to dig myself into. Einar's promise to pull me out is a small, burning light in the darkness. It promises to light up my entire soul and fill me with warmth again, if only so that I can hold on for just a little while longer.

The mission to speak to the Volva was an important step in reaching our goal, and had a better outcome than expected. I believe it was due to the fact that it had only consisted of brothers, and Stellan had been there. Not even the Volva or those woods could shake my little brother. It would be the last time all the brothers would go on a mission together. It was dangerous, and Einar couldn't afford a misstep from bringing another. We've been through a lot, but we're still mostly human. The brothers are still most at ease in the company of each other. Only brothers can be trusted. Not others.

I look at the group of others on the beach and see Anders wave at me with the arm whose hand I had bitten off. I pray that Mads can talk Einar out of leaving me alone with them.

"No." Einar replies sternly. "We are not here to raid. We are here to be better, to create better. To build something of our own, something good, something great. We do that by getting what we came here for in the wood successfully, as instructed by the Volva. We leave the village alone."

I can tell Mads is wounded by the chastising, and I think Einar can as well.

"I need you both in the positions I have designated because you have my trust. It's past dusk now, and I plan to have us setting back out by dawn on this ship if we are successful in there."

He turns, looks at me, and says, "No one goes to the village. The men need to be ready to push off at a moment's notice, help carry any wounded out, and provide cover as we come out. I can only spare one brother, and it must be a brother who can handle something this important. We need this ship to be ready when we come out in the morning. I need you, Bjorn. No one else. You. You must do this for the brothers. For Stellan, not just for me. For us. For our future. A future where we never have to do these things again. A future where the past can't touch us or weigh us down anymore. It's okay." He grabs Mads shoulder as well and firmly squeezes both shoulders reassuringly. "You can trust my words to you."

All my negative emotions die down, the seeds of doubt and fear that had started to sprout once again wilt under the weight of his words as I surrender to his speech. I do trust his words, but I do not trust the men he is leaving me behind with.

We need at least twelve men to be able to sail back. I do not know what is in the wood, but if any man were to die it is likely to be in there. I want to tell him to take some of the expendable men into the wood with him and leave a few brothers here with me to protect the ship from any unknowns. To protect the brothers' numbers, in case what they may encounter ends up being too much.

You should always bring a cow with you. That is what his father taught us. Bring a cow with you, and should you be chased by a wolf, you have something to give it to buy you distance between yourself and the wolf. That debt has helped us before in battle. I know why he refuses it. He wants to live now as if the world we're building is here now as much as possible. No cows. It's not worth bringing up to him, he'll shut me down, but still.

"Einar, leave Mads here with me and take three of the others."

"Three? Shit, it would take at least six of them to replace me, but three would be enough to buy you time should you encounter anything in there."

I shoot Mads a warning look, but he catches on too late; Einar is already giving us a look, making us feel desperate to make up for disappointing him.

"In the new world, there will be no cows, Bjorn. It's time you learn to live without them. Using them only brings out worse."

I lower my eyes and look down as he releases his hand from my shoulder. Just like that, the comfort is gone, leaving only numbness where his hand was. Guilt washes over me. I know the debt I have, but it is his father's fault, a fault he has inherited. On one hand he speaks of how the price of life is death, but on the other he preaches the importance of not being wasteful with spending for the creation of the new life we are building. We have already spent so much.

My hand moves independently, and I am clutching the dark heart stone again, wishing Stellan was here. He is the only brother not on this trip. Einar had sent him away on his own to retrieve a heart from a place of sand and sun, another task given by Grandmother Volva that night.

As much as I love Mads, Stellan is truly the only one I feel safe with, and the only one who can temporarily alleviate the darkness of my hugr. My thoughts seem less intense when he is around. When I feel I am about to lose myself, drowning hopelessly, Stellan always has a way of pulling me up and making me breathe air. I would have happily traded any good fortune the Hamingja assured us to have him here. I wish Einar would see that he doesn't need the luck he is chasing when he has all of us with him.

The Hamingja was given to him from his father right before he died. Somehow Einar had convinced him to let him take her to the next battle after we had met a severe loss at the last one. As soon as his father consented and she was with Einar, he swiftly pulled a dagger out and placed it into his father's heart. There seemed to be no love lost from the girl to his father. The Hamingja seemed already determined to affix to Einar's fate and bring luck to his cause.

I think she was weary of the endless war and destruction without a promise of ending or rebirth as much as we were. A united country didn't mean much if the country died in the process of uniting it. Death is the price of life, that is truth as much as life being a debt.

I remember his speech that night. He had said all this cannot end in death. To die in glory for what? To end up in another great hall where we wait for another battle, a final battle that is not for us and that we are destined to lose anyways. All this death must amount to good, not bad. Uniting the country would never happen, as his father planned poorly. The limited fields we had suitable for farming had mostly been battle ruined. Even if they hadn't been, most of those able to farm have died, leaving us unable to provide enough.

He told us there was another way, a way to make all this have meaning. Death is the price of life. New life. But he said that was okay, it was good. We could take it in order to start again somewhere else that was better; a place with waters and lands that were flowing and fertile. It would cost us greatly, but it would amount to something for all of us. He said he had taken the first death that night for this new nation. His fathers' life. He asked that we all join him, together. That we would fight and build something good. Something better. Something for everyone.

I remember looking at the Hamingja as he spoke that night, the light in her eyes dancing in a way that mimicked the night sky lights on clear days. She was beautiful, with pale skin that subtly illuminated in the slightest darkness. Her hair was glowing radiantly, as if she was a distant descendant of Thor's wife, the goddess Sif, and had inherited her golden hair.

Thinking back on that night, I am sure she is the reason Einar's speech won over the entire army and he was able to settle peacefully with his father's foes. She became a part of him that night. Liberated from his father, she shined more brightly than we had ever seen her shine before. Looking at her now, though, broken and dim, I cannot help but feel as though Einar, and maybe our luck, has run out. I fear we may lose on this island in that wood. I wonder if Volva knew that this would happen.

I've gone over my own death in my head many times. It's an intrusive vision that runs in my head. The best version, the one I hope for, needs Stellan. I do not fear death; I know Hel is waiting for me. I just want to say goodbye to Stellan properly before I go, especially since we were not given the chance to do so with Father, or Mother, or the others. I would pray to see him again, that he finds success in his task and is able to bring the heart back to Einar. But the gods do not listen to help us, they only listen to help themselves. It is hard to know the will of the gods. Is the voice guiding Einar that of the All Father, or that of the trickster? We cannot know.

Einar walks towards the beach where the brothers and others have assembled in two distinct groups. The night is about to begin, and he is getting them all ready for the tasks ahead.

"Well, fuck," Mads says, grabbing his axe from his belt and walking away to take his place with the brothers on the beach, leaving me with the Hamingja.

I should follow him to address the others. I can feel them staring at me, probably fantasizing about throwing a spear in my back once the brothers have left. I have not shown them any respect or hid my distaste for them on this journey, and do not plan to start now. The large, loud one called Anders particularly annoys me and has made no attempt to veil his opinion of me. He has told the others that I am too old and impotent when it comes to battle to lead or make decisions on anything, much less them.

He is of the old mindset, despite his age, as are most of the others. Caught up in the idea of the glory of taking and living in the moment, gaining glory, and resurrecting the old ways rather than building a new way. It's funny, considering they weren't around during the supposed glory of the old days. They are reminiscing over a time they were never part of. Yet they defend the idea of it as if they were there at the very beginning. They refuse to acknowledge that they stand to benefit the most from the new way and world we are building. I shouldn't let them get to me as much as they do.

"Mads," I say, calling him back to me before he leaves with Einar for the wood line.

I clutch the dark heart stone around my neck in my hand. I struggle with it, torn between waving him away and giving him the necklace, as if it could assure his return from the woods, and his return back to me. The idea of parting with it fills me with anxiety, but the idea of being left here on this beach without any brothers come dawn scares me even more. Stellan had said it could lead me through the darkness. Maybe it can actually work for Mads in those woods. He is more worthy than me. Mads, always adept at reading me and my thoughts, places his hand over mine that lies over my chest, clutching the stone.

"It'll be alright, little brother," he says.

Suddenly, I am lifted off the ground, being crushed by the giant arms encircling me in a painful bear hug.

"I'll miss you too, but it won't be for long. I promise I won't leave you alone to deal with those assholes for too long."

Releasing me after placing a hard kiss on my cheek, he turns to make his way back towards the woods with Einar and the brothers.

He calls over his shoulder, "No offense, but you have terrible taste in jewelry anyways." Giggling, he walks away.

Like Stellan, Mads is always strong. I am always weak, unable to even part with a piece of jewelry. I clutch it even harder in my hand, willing it to lead me, to show me the way. I turn and walk back to the Hamingja. As I get closer, I can see the light hovering over her body, making its way back to the sky.

Ionna

The Village

14

NO TIME FOR FORGIVENESS

As my shaky hands place the blood-stained whale-bone needle and Naia's coat on the table, I rise. Quietly, I make my way to the door, carefully opening it and slipping out, leaving my husband to carefully untangle himself from the slumbering limbs of our children. It's dark outside despite the full moon, which should be shining brightly but appears dim, as if trying not to draw attention to itself. The wind suddenly pulls like a silent dramatic gasp before gently releasing. I can see along with it that a faint smoky light I have never witnessed before is streaming from the beach beyond the rocky outcropping that separates our village from it. Everything seems to stand still, suspended in time, including me.

I watch the light turn brighter as it enters the dark sky. It begins to move like a dance to a tune only it can hear against the backdrop of the faint moonlight and clouds. Heavy footsteps and breathing come up the path to the village, breaking the trance the strange lights had put me in. Peeling my eyes from the sky, I can see the welcome outline of Daithí's muscular body coming towards me. I point back to the sky as he comes to stand beside me, and we watch the stream of light finishing its ascension.

When I return my gaze from the sky, I notice my husband has joined us outside the hut. He was never a fan of Daithí. He looks at us both with a serious, concerned expression on his face.

"What was that?" he asks us.

"They're here," I say, looking back up at the sky to see the lights slowly dissipate into the darkness.

"We need to get the children, and their coats." I peel my eyes back to the earth, a sense of urgency flooding back over me.

I turn to move back towards the hut when my husband blocks my path with his body.

"The children are asleep. I'll not have you waking them. Not until you tell me what's going on." He says, gesturing to the sky and Daithí.

"Tell you what's going on?"

Anger rises in my voice as I try to shoulder past him. He tries to grab my arm, but I dodge his grasp, turning on him with long suppressed rage.

"I have been telling you what's going on and you have refused to listen!"

"Ionna," Daithí says, reaching his hand out, trying to calm me down.

"Don't tell me you've fallen for her nonsense, Daithí?" my husband sneers.

"Nonsense?" I say, my voice trembling as I try to lower it and not wake the children. I feel as though I could kill him myself right now.

"The only nonsense in this house was your excuses for not saving our son. Our baby. You and your people, they stood in my way once already, and it cost me a child; one that I have not yet given up on despite all these years, unlike you. I will not let you stand in my way this time. Go ahead and stand to the side. That's what you do best when our children's lives are at risk."

He looks down silently, and I burn with satisfaction and justice.

"I don't have time for you," I say coldly, triumphantly.

I move to walk around him when I feel Daithí's hand on my shoulder, holding me back.

"Ionna," Daithí says, "You can't come back once you cross."

"What?" I ask, turning back to Daithí.

"You can't come back, Ionna." my husband says.

I turn to see him looking at me with tear-filled eyes and a face rolling with emotion. I look for Daithí's face and see his gaze pointed to the ground, his right foot moving awkwardly in the earth.

"Daithí?" I ask, my hand raising slightly out towards him.

"Did he not fully explain it to you, then?" He asks bitterly, wiping away tears before pointing to Daithí.

"You are her husband, why did you not explain?" Daithí asks, not lifting his gaze.

"Explain what?" I ask.

"The reason why you can't come back. What they do to those who try." My husband says, taking another step towards me, his face shifting to a hate-filled sneer.

"You ever notice the old wooden poles in the middle of the village? The ones standing in scarred earth? No? I didn't imagine so; you don't pay attention to much around you besides the sea and your lover. Oh yes, I know what you have been up to while you leave our children to the care of your so-called family. A family that is so great, yet you supposedly left them to come here to this place of death and misfortune by your words and actions.

"Those poles, those are where they take the ones who try to come back. They tie them. They burn them. They say those who come back aren't really loved ones. They're changed, substitutes from the other folk sent to trick us. But by their screams, Ionna, you would never be able to tell the difference."

His face changes from one emotion to the next, turbulent as storm winds as I stare at him in horror, the realization dawning on me. Knowing now the reason why my husband stopped. Why Daithí and the other villager prevented me from going in after Cael, from crossing myself and trying to bring us both back. They were trying to save me, to save us from being burned alive.

"But you came back?" I turn back to Daithí.

It can't be true, because Daithí is here. He crossed to look for Cael and made it back. He would not have lied to me. He wouldn't have kept something like that from me.

"You said you went back to look for him that day?" I ask him, taking a cautious step towards him, needing to see the eyes that he is so firmly keeping planted to the ground.

"Daithí? You said you went to the woods but didn't find him?" I ask again, but I receive no response.

The horrible truth becomes glaringly obvious. I want to ignore it; I want him to look at me and tell me it's not true. I want him to be what I had believed he was, what I needed him to be. I want to push away the tearing in my heart and soul that screams everything was all a lie. You. Him. Everything.

"You didn't go back?" I ask, my voice shaking as I fight back the urge to release the sounds of sorrow and heartbreak building inside me.

"No, I did go back to look for him," he says, finally looking up, his eyes wide.

"I, I just didn't cross. I did search for him though, Ionna. You have to believe me, please," he continues.

"For what purpose, Daithí?" Cian asks. "You would have brought him back to burn?!" My husband yells as he rushes forward, knocking Daithí to the ground.

I should tell him to stop. As they tussle on the ground, I should yell at them to quit with their foolishness. Remind them we don't have time, but I remain frozen in place watching them.

"No! No, I—" he starts to say as he struggles to push Cian off of him while trying to avoid the hits from his fists, but he is cut off by another round of urgent barking from the Seals below.

The shrill barks wake me up inside and bring my husband and lover out of their scuffle. The disappointment, the betrayal, it will have to wait. Panic sets in again, dominating my other emotions, and I remember my children. I remember that I am here for my children, they are my purpose. I turn back to my husband.

"Cian. Plea..."

Before I can finish, the barking of the Seals is replaced by loud, chaotic noises from across the village.

Screams continue to grow louder, and we all start to smell smoke.

The children's cries and calls for us from inside the hut join the frightening chorus coming from the village. My husband pushes himself off of Daithí, wiping a small smear of blood from his hand on to his shirt as he runs back into the cottage for the children. A bloodied Daithí and I follow close behind.

"Ionna…" Daithí tries to talk to me as we enter the threshold, but I cut him off.

"Don't," I say, unable to look at him.

My husband grabs our eldest first, handing Caden to me as I stand by the table and hearth. He frantically starts dressing him in the first crude coat as Caden sucks in his lip, trying to be brave and hide his tears.

"Daaa," Caden whimpers.

"Get dressed, now…" My husband tells him firmly, reaching to place his outstretched hand on our son's head.

"What can I do?" Daithí asks, but I still can't bear to look or speak to him.

My husband hands him our daughter, who remains silent. Cian puts aside his hatred in this moment for the sake of our children. I turn to grab our younger son, but my husband is already dressing him in his coat while kissing his face, trying to comfort him as he sobs and fights my husband's attempts.

"No! I don't want too! Momma!" Aidan yells, reaching for me, and my heart breaks, the tears flow freely, and I can't stop them.

As my husband wrestles with Aidan's unwilling arms as he calls for me, I look at where I dropped the needle and Naia's incomplete coat, panicking. I pick it up, and the needle swings from the opening of the unfinished sleeve. There is no more time. I look at my husband with tears in my eyes, but he does not meet them, still focused on Aidan. There is no time to process the confessions. No time to apologize. No time to forgive either of us.

Cian grabs Naia from Daithí's arms and takes a now-dressed Aidan by the hand as he leads all three children out of the house and to the entrance of the hidden path. The path the children and I had so often taken down to the beach from the side of our house. The path that once led to cheerful playdates with my family now leads to my children's only chance for survival.

I grab the needle and tiny coat with its undone sleeve and finally look at Daithí, who places a hand on my shoulder, but I no longer feel any warmth from it.

"I'm sorry, Ionna. I know it doesn't matter now, and I've no time to explain myself. But I'm sorry."

I look for his eyes, but they have moved on from me and come to settle on my husband's fishing spears and nets. He grabs two spears and follows Cian and the children out. I stand for a moment in the hut, alone. All the emotions that had been bursting inside me all these years, filling me with love, and grief, and hope and hate have abandoned me in this moment. I stand in the empty house one last time feeling a strange complete emptiness I have never felt before. As if everything I had been feeling all these years, and what I felt tonight broke me to where I am unable to feel anything ever again. For a moment I am unsure if there is anything left in me.

"Momma!" I hear a fearful tiny voice yell from outside.

"Hurry!" I hear the shrill barking from my family down below.

"Ionna!" I hear the voices of the men I once loved call in unison.

Small flickers from my dark and hollow inside come to life. I force myself to move again. One foot in front of the other. There has been so much betrayal on this land, from me and to me. I will not continue it any longer. The flickers ignite into flames as I move towards the open door. I will not betray my children; I will not betray myself.

I step outside. My husband is already talking to the boys as my daughter clings to him, hiding her face, no longer silent as she cries. Our oldest sniffles through his brave face and nods his head at the words from my husband. He grabs his younger brother's hand, and they head down the path together. I walk up to my husband and our daughter, my hands shaking and turning white from the force of gripping the coat and needle so tightly. He pries her tiny hands from around his neck as she cries "No, daddy." and hands her to me as she fights to stay with him. I grab her and hold her tightly to my chest, the coat and needle still in one hand. He grabs my face with both hands and kisses me, and it feels like forgiveness, for both of us.

"I will not tell you to be brave, to be strong, to not cry." His hands fall to mine, and we hold Naia's coat together.

"You are more than just a girl. This is more than just a coat. It has to be. You must be." His eyes are red with the strain of holding back tears again.

I cry at his words.

"I will not get in the way anymore when it comes to saving our children," he says.

He gives me one last kiss before he pushes me roughly towards the path and heads back to the hut. He walks to Daithí who hands him a spear. He accepts it silently before heading towards the village without another look back at us.

"Ionna," Daithí says softly as he comes to me, reaching his hand out.

But I can't bear to look at him, so I turn away, no longer knowing if I love or hate him. Disappointed that our great love didn't live up in the end. Naia's soft cries against the increasingly loud ones from the village bring me back to the moment and I start to walk down the path. I feel him grab my arm tightly and press something cold and hard against my hand. I look and see a bleached whalebone knife like the one from the story.

"I would still follow you down any path that you would let me."

I take the knife but don't look at him, still raw from his betrayal.

"Take care of our daughter," is the last thing he says to me.

I want to say something to him, but I don't know what. Standing amongst the smoke and growing sounds of violence from the village I know the time has passed. There isn't any time left for explanations or forgiveness. Our sons are already almost to the beach below when I finally look back over my shoulder to try to see Daithí or my husband. But I can't see them through the barrier Daithí must have created at the path entrance after we parted. All I can see is the glowing lights from large fires and the rising smoke coming from them. The screams are all the same when they burn, my husband's words make me shudder as the screams rise from the village along with the smoke. Our daughter is quiet again, burying her face into my chest as I race towards our sons and onto the beach.

The boys have stopped a few feet away from the shallow surf, where a few of my kin in human form, led by my sister, are already waiting for them. The questions I had pondered weeks ago on the beach on that last sunny day of carefree play have been answered. She has the same long, dark hair, the same face as pale as mine had once been.

Behind Aine's pale, naked body inside her open coat I can see more of our kin bobbing in the waves out ahead. They are quiet now, no more barking. No more songs of warning. No more time to look back upon the past and path that has led me and my children here.

The time is now.

EINAR

THE WOODS

15

INTO THE WOODS

"Remember, fair, honored, respected, loved one, should you utter one hint of a scream, if one part of you is afraid in there, you will never ascend to feast in the great halls with your fathers, with your brothers." The Hamingja's words stay with me as we stand upon the wood line.

But I knew early on no good death waited for me. No great hall filled with my father's ancestors and other great warriors who had died fearlessly in battle. Father had me thrown in the pits with a she-bear, wild and frenzied. No weapons, just me. I think he had hoped this would finally make me change. That it would prove I was not only supreme, but one of them. I was, after all, half-born of a she-bear and Father in his attempt to engineer a general of his blood like no other. It worked in some ways, as I was his only son. Something Mother, the Queen, did not appreciate. As the bear raged in the cage in the pits, I knew I would not change. I couldn't. It didn't matter how hard I tried, or wanted to, I couldn't will it to happen.

Father's men baited her with long spears, and the clatter of swords on shields, enraging her. Desperate, I looked around for anything to use as a weapon. I finally found a loose metal bar at the top of the pit holding cell I was in and pulled it down, creating a makeshift spear. They opened the gate, and I knew I had to run forward; Father was watching. They were all watching. I knew I was going to die, and I was scared.

There was no good death waiting for me, no Valhalla. My place was not with the warriors who welcomed death. Who waited eagerly for the last great battle at the end of days. The she-bear turned around, giant paw raised to strike, but when she saw me, she paused. I took the opportunity to rush the broken shaft with all my might into her chest. She stood for a few minutes, with a strange look on her scarred face as the crowd cheered and my brothers whimpered. As she fell to her knees she transformed into the form of a woman, naked, wounded. Her raised hand slowly lowered to point, no, reach for me. Her last breath rattled out, "Einar Thorasson."

"Mother?" The word cried out in my heart, the word whispered on my lips.

Her lips twitched into an attempted smile from my recognition as tears fell first, and her body after. No,

I was not meant for the good death; I was meant for the good life. For my mother, for my brothers, for my people. Control. Bury the emotions, control them. I walked to her lifeless body, pressed my hand into the wound I dealt, took her blood with shaking fingers, with raging emotions inside of me that I was struggling to suppress, and marked my face. I threw my hands up and looked up at Father, who smirked. As the crowd cheered loudly, the youngest of the brothers whimpered in their cages. We both knew I failed, but he still got his desired result.

There is no looking back. No signs of weakness, just like that day in the pits. We have made it this far, and I feel like we are so close to reaching the end game. The Hamingja is surely lying dead where we left her against the boat, and with her, so is a part of me, a weakness reserved for those unfit to lead. I no longer have to bear it, to bear her like I did my father and, for a fleeting moment, my mother. The only comfort is knowing that Bjorn with his soft touch is there with Freyda as her light goes out.

The tree line is dark. Some of them have asked about torches, but they will only hinder our journey. The Volva's words were clear. I swear I can still feel them pressed against my ear, speaking of my destiny, of my triumph.

"In darkness you must enter, from darkness you must return. In the darkness you will find the answer that will lead you to a light that is your own, that you created. Turn the cold, dark heart of a monster and the path you seek for you and your people will be created," she had said with lips as red as life blood. With lips that burned hot against my ears like the fire in a forge. She was the air fanning the fire of creation. I would be the smith that created beauty and strength from the raw materials of the earth.

"Einar, the only one getting any prettier by the minute is me, should we go?" Mads smart mouth comes ringing through the darkness, making some of the brother's chuckle, and some of them groan.

I had appreciated him more in our youth, and his ability to raise the spirits of the men. To rally them when need be. As we've come closer to our goal, his mouth has become harder for me to tolerate.

"Mads, Leif, turn now and take the front," I command.

I hear Mads take a heavy sigh at having to undress out of his beloved garments and adornments. He is the only one of my men who is fond of all the pretty things. Of nice clothing, bright jewels, and beautiful lovers. He is the largest of the berserkers, then Bjorn, who is waiting with the ship and the other men.

"So much for picking the right outfit for the occasion," Mads quips, neatly folding his long tunic and trousers, stacking them on top of each other and placing his golden necklaces, cuffs and rings in between. Naked in the moonlight, he walks over to an old, knotted root of an oak tree protruding from the ground and gently places his clothing next to it.

"Mads, weren't you the one who said black goes with everything?" cracks Ulf, one of the smaller of my men.

Mads replies in a growl I interpret to mean "Fuck off," as he transforms into a great black bear and the men chuckle quietly.

Leif transforms next, a dark brown bear. A tuft of white hair on his chest and around his neck almost glows in the dark. It will make it easier to spot him up ahead as we enter. Leif stands up on his hind legs and starts sniffing the air cautiously before coming back to all fours.

"Let's move," I command, and we enter in rows of two into the dark tree line.

It's dark in the woods, as dark as the northern forest where we sought the Volva. As dangerous as that journey had been, this seems to be more so. Maybe because there is more at stake.

"Follow the path to a place where three rivers become one. Listen for the song of the washerwoman, and in a spring not far from the river you will find her," the Volva had said. As we enter, no path can be seen. No river, either. Carefully, we step into the foliage, mindfully placing our feet, one arm feeling our way forward, one ready to defend. The branches of the fyrre trees that parted so easily for Leif grab at me, pulling on anything they can land a grip on as if to hold me back, to prevent me from entering. The hole that should have been created when Leif first entered is nonexistent. As if the wood welcomed him in like family but did not grant me the same grace. As if it senses only the animal in him and only the man in me.

We walk in silence, with just the noise of our breath and the movement of the woods against us announcing our intrusion. It feels unnatural, that the woods would be so quiet. No animals, no creaking trees or branches.

After a short while, we come into a small clearing with enough room for us to group together. Leif, still in the front leading the way, stops at the entrance of what looks to be an old cart path. The path is remarkably clear from overgrowth, as if still traveled daily. How is that possible? I see no other entrance to the clearing. I can't imagine the villagers come down this way, based on their village's location. Maybe there's another village?

There is a feeling of uneasiness in the air. Leif's ears, which were cocked forward as we entered, now suddenly flatten against his large, blocky head. I move to his side and see a large black cat with a white patch on its chest sitting on the path a few feet in from the clearing. It's a peculiar sight, one that does not sit well with me. Did I misjudge the landing and place our entrance too near a village? The Volva had only mentioned one.

The animal looks much larger than a normal barn cat. Suddenly Leif makes a short burst forward towards the animal, slapping the ground with his heavy paw before backing away again. The feline is unfazed as it continues to gaze upon us, feigning interest. Leif again bursts forward, slapping at the ground. Blowing and clacking his teeth this time, but the animal again displays no interest. I place my hand on Leif's back to calm him. It's unusual for him to show this type of uneasiness, and it sends a wave through the brothers, infecting all with his agitation.

"Leif," I call calmly as my hand presses down against his back.

Suddenly, we are all frozen in place, yet the feline continues to switch its tail back and forth as it watches us. The black cat takes one look at me with eyes that seems to glow unnaturally in the darkness before sauntering off the path and disappearing into the foliage and trees. Once it is gone, we regain our mobility. Mads walks up, pushing those in his way as he comes to Leif, knocking his teeth and open mouth against Leif's muzzle until Leif returns back in same. Huffing, Mads takes the lead, and the rest follow.

We are not long down the dirt cart path when a breeze suddenly pushes through the trees, causing all of us to stop in our tracks. Mads stands on his hind legs and sniffs the air with his great big muzzle. The breeze pulls back, and the dark forest surrounding us erupts into noise, bursting to life. Calls and cackling of beings in the night sound from all directions. Two more men suddenly change form, bursting out of their clothes, weapons falling to the ground.

"Easy now!" I command.

I don't know what has gotten into them to lose their form so. They're all battle-hardened. I know this is worse for them than the trek into the dark forest the night we sought the Volva, but I did not expect a single one of them to lose their form as they are now. These woods, this mission, is spooking my men more than anything we have encountered before. I fear that I may lose my control on them if we stay here too long. They act like boys facing battle for the first time.

Mads again lets out a huff and turns around with his large open mouth, banging his teeth amongst the snouts of the others who had turned, rallying them back into control, into submission. No sooner have the men calmed down, then a blood curdling scream rings out against the large knotty trees up ahead. Another man transforms, and I am left standing with more bears and fewer men. Again, I call out to the brothers.

"Easy now, hold your forms!"

I take the lead, and Mads comes up beside me, with one nod of his large head we step forward together down the path. Slowly we walk, setting the pace for the men behind us. We've gone maybe another hundred feet or so before the dark outline of a large, ruined building begins to peek out overhead. Huffs come from behind me, followed by a low growl from Mads, signaling to the others to stay alert, to stay calm.

Fifty more feet, and the black cat appears again, cutting us off on the path. Once again, we are frozen in place, statues on the path as everything else continues to move around us freely. The cat once again saunters off, and as we regain our mobility, a woman's laughter comes cackling from behind us. I see Mads turn around abruptly while I stay forward, locked on where the feline just was. The laughter stops, and I hear a yell and the sound of large paws pushing violently from the ground and the crashing of a large beast's body through the woods.

"Kell!!" I hear Ulf yell.

"Fuck!" Ulf yells, running in after him.

"Everyone on me!" I command, turning back around at the sound of the woman's cackle to the front of us. This time the cat does not appear.

We are down two brothers, but I can't afford to wait on Ulf and Kell to return.

"Let's go," I say, pushing the men forward.

"Be on your guard and stay on the path together! If someone leaves do *not* follow."

The path takes us closer to the ruined building ahead, which is beginning to look more like and old guard tower. I can only imagine a ruined castle or village lay beyond it. I push the thought of what other horrors fill the ruins out of my head. As we near, an intoxicating smell wafts from a small deer path on the right side of the trail. It fills my head with a thick fog, making my thinking and movement feel much slower. The smell beckons me to abandon my mission and follow it down the harmless deer path, but I ignore it and push forward.

"Keep going!" I yell to my men, but the words feel as though I am speaking to them underwater, such is the power of the smell that challenges me to resist.

I stop by the entrance of the trail, unwilling, unable to lose any more men. I push them past it as I see them each struggling with themselves to ignore it. The scent muddles my brain, like having too much drink. I shake my head as if I can dispel the scent, shake the haziness it causes me out. Each man and bear I push forward makes me feel as though I'm pushing myself closer to the trail and to losing out to the desire to go down it.

A quiet song begins, coming from the small path that appears not as dark as its surroundings. Haunting, beautiful. It works against us with the scent to break down our will and come to it. There is one more brother to get past it, and then I can leave as well. Arne comes to the trail head and stops, his big bear head pushing me out of the way to look down it.

"No, Arne." I try to push him back and turn his brown blocky head back to the path, but I can't budge him when he's in this form. He sniffs and lets out a few huffs before starting a slow lumber down the small trail.

"Arne!" I call again, shaking my head to try and clear the thick cloud that tries to penetrate my thoughts. Looking after him, I can see someone at the end of the trail, whose song and scent is seducing us. The being that calls us to it is beautiful. Though I cannot tell if it is a man or a woman, I desire it all the same. The desire threatens to overtake me, and I force myself to look away as an involuntary groan escapes my throat.

Looking down I make one last attempt to stop him. "Arne," I say weakly, but I know he is lost. I force myself to move away from the path before I, too, am lost to it. The number of our lost or fallen brothers is now three, and our expedition has only just begun in this dangerous wood. As we get further down the path, further from the seductive side trail, the singing gets fainter, and the smell begins to dissipate. We walk quietly and I know I am steadily losing my grasp on my men, on my mission. If I am not more careful, I will also lose myself.

"Brothers... "

Suddenly a short, loud yelp in the distance is heard, and I know in my heart that it is Arne, and that he is gone. I am frozen in place temporarily until I can push the feelings back down inside. I can't lose control. I have to succeed. I will succeed.

I know the men have all heard it too, and they all look at me, human and bear faces alike. I see in their eyes they are unsure. Even Mads, who doesn't move to rally the men this time.

"It's just up ahead, Brothers. *Stay. Together*," I say.

I once again move to the front to take the lead, pulling out my dagger for them to see, a show, a reminder to put up their guards. There will be no more sleeping, no more distractions on this trip.

We move quickly on the path, and soon come upon the ruined tower. Behind it lies a small river with the three branches, as the Volva had said. I raise my hands to silence the men, though they are quiet already, and

I listen. Beyond the babbling of the water, I can hear the faint, sad song of a woman. It's there, coming from the middle branch. I motion for my men to follow me as I start towards the bank of the river, looking for a point to cross the swift flowing water. Our silence and progress are halted by the sound of a small giggle, like that of a child.

"Steady." I tell my men and motion for them to continue forward.

"Now, where did you come from, child?"

I turn to see Mads back in his human form, crouching down with a borrowed blue tunic around his waist like a skirt, calling the child to him.

The child, no more than two, smiles with a face of innocence. His curly dark hair frames his large black eyes. Something seems off about the child, but I can't quite place it.

"Mads, stop," I warn.

"Come here now child, are you lost?" Mads continues to speak to the child, coaxing it to come nearer and ignoring me.

"Mads," I say again.

Turning to me he says, "Let's see where he came from. Maybe there is a village near by that you didn't account for. We need to know."

Mads reaches his hand out to the small child who responds with another giggle and steps back towards the brush next to the tower he had emerged from. Mads stands up and takes slow steps towards the boy, so as not to frighten him, not picking up on the strangeness of the babe. Mads has always had a fondness for children, trying to save them when he could. He never said so, but it always seemed as though he desired one of his own, something that was not possible for him. The child turns around and runs into the thicket with speed that seems unnatural for one of that age. Before I can say anything, Mads is already disappearing into the thicket after him.

Fuck. Four brothers are now lost to us, and we haven't even reached the washerwoman yet. I can see the men are spooked. They too have done the math and know what losses we have taken in such a short time. Without Mads, I am not sure how I will keep them rallied, keep them calm. As I begin to lose control and spiral along with my men, I hear the faint singing of a woman again, and I know it is the washerwoman. It has to be her. I know that we are close. I know I will succeed as I regain my control.

"Keep pushing forward. Keep fighting against the wood. Do not follow it into folly as the others have. Our hope, the hope of our people, lies ahead. It lies in your ability to stay in control and follow my orders. Listen, men, and you can hear the old hag's song. We are close. We need to keep pushing," I say.

"Do not let fear control you!" I repeat one of father's favorite sayings in an attempt to calm them.

"Einar!" I hear Holger call from the ruined tower. He must have checked it out, while we were distracted by the child.

"There is an old bridge here, or what remains of it," he says.

I walk over to see him taking a cautious step onto the remnants of a crumbling old stone bridge covered in moss, testing his weight out on it. One side remains intact, with the middle part crumbling and large chunks missing from the other side. I nod my head at him as he looks to me before taking another step, and then another until he successfully makes it across. Leif, still in bear form stands guard as I cross next, then Ralph, then Olaf, and Kare, until the only ones left to cross are Leif, Gunnar, and Iver in their bear form.

Iver goes first, and the bridge groans under his weight. He crosses hastily, and stones crumble underneath him as he does. Gunnar is next, causing more of the bridge to crumble. Leif is the only one left standing on the other side of the narrow river. He takes one step, and the bridge begins to crumble even more, causing him to step back on the bank. He looks up at me and then begins to pace back and forth in front of the bridge.

"Stay back and look for another way to cross," I call to him from the other side. "Should this bridge crumble we will need another way."

Leif lets out a loud huff and continues to pace, clearly displeased at the prospect of staying behind alone. We haven't the time to discuss, though, and we're all eager to see this task finished and make our way out of the wood. With the river now crossed, we move towards the stream in the middle that feeds into it, where the faint song of the woman was heard. As we near it, I again stop the men and bid them to quiet down so I can listen.

The river and the song lead us to another old ruin, this one much larger than the old tower. It looks to be the remains of what was once a great stone house. Large moss and vine covered grey stone walls are mostly still standing, but with a roof that is only partially still up. As we near it, I can see that some of the stones are stained with the brown rust color of old, forgotten blood, as if painted and sealed with it.

The woman's voice is nearer, and I can hear the water flowing and the splashing of her chore in a nearby spring. I can now make out that her song is a mournful dirge for those I assume have died or are yet to. I motion for the men to stay behind and stay quiet as I lay down my weapons and crouch on the ground to silently creep up to her as she is consumed with her task.

Squat and ugly, the woman who is more nightmare creature than woman bends over, occupied with her washing as the Volva had said she would be. Her long, grotesque breasts each hang over a shoulder, occasionally falling forward in her way, making her stop and curse as she flings the floppy and uncooperative appendage back over her shoulder again. A putrid smell wafts in the air. Milk dribbling out of her gnarled nipples and running down along her back must be the source of it.

My stomach turns multiple times inside me. I fight the urge to vomit at the task ahead of me. The Volva had said I must take her by surprise, crawling up and suckling on her breast, pretending to be a foster child in order to gain the answers that I seek from her. For the answers to build my new world. A world in my image, and not my father's.

I crawl low on the ground, using my arms to pull me silently forward until I am a mere foot from her back and putrid breasts. The milk drip, drip, dripping down her boney back puddles in the dips and dents of her rib cage that protrudes through her thin, sagging skin. This is it, the moment of the final test to prove my worth. To prove I have what it takes to be a leader of a new world, a better leader and better world than that of my father.

Stealing myself against the task, I shoot like a snake in the grass and grab the monster's teat with my hand, quickly shoving it in my mouth to suckle as hard and aggressive as a young calf that has just been reunited with its mother after a long separation. Though the smell is horrendous, the taste is a surprising mixture of sweet and sour fermentation. Like a strong mead, the milk goes straight to my head, and my thoughts begin to tingle and buzz as the old crone speaks.

"Come now, child, who suckles on me so as I do my work?"

"It is I, your child," I say before continuing to suckle as the crone chuckles.

"Tell me now child, what is it you want that you bother me so and interrupt my work?"

Once again taking her breast out of my mouth but keeping a firm grip on it, I ask her the questions that have been burning in me since we met the Volva.

BJORN

THE WOODSIDE BEACH
&
THE VILLAGE

16

BURY WHAT IS LOST

The show is over. The girl now lays beneath a layer of carefully placed sand that my giant paws swept over her. I stand, stunned, on all fours, panting from the exertion of fighting the sand to dig a grave unworthy of the host that had been the bearer of what I had just seen. How, when I looked back at the girl on the ground after Einar left, her chest was no longer straining, no longer moving up and down as she breathed. The only thing moving in her lifeless body was the light that was dimly lit in her eyes a few moments ago.

How the light was rising out of them like smoke. How it moved so vibrantly, so beautifully as it rose from her into the night sky, a stark contrast to its former host. A stark contrast to every violent, dark, dirty death I had always caused or witnessed previously.

I'm not sure why, but I was moved to take a step back as the light continued to leave her, as if to give it more room to breathe as it danced its way to the night sky. It joined the full moon above, which seemed to dim in honor of the light rising up to join it.

Such a small amount seemed to have remained in the Hamingja as she lay dying moments before. The small amount that has finished leaving her eyes and left her completely void of life or light had grown larger, more vibrant, as it finished leaving her body and moved upward in a steady stream. When her light finally reached the sky, it continued its final dance before fading away, leaving the sky dark except for the moon, still dimly lit as if it were now in mourning for its brief companion.

I can't help but think about what this is costing us. What it cost the Hamingja, who is now nothing more than another poor dead girl, poorly buried beneath a layer of foreign sand. Tears form in my eyes and my breath catches, my paws tremble. The seeds of doubt and fear are now in full bloom within my heart. I have seen a lot of death, caused a lot of death. Hers was the most beautiful, but it has left me feeling empty of any hope in this moment. I will never stop feeling this way.

She was our luck, and we used her up until her light couldn't bear to reside in its vessel any longer. Just as Einar's father has used up my people until no more of us could be made, and those who remain dwindle. A sign, maybe, that we and our cause are unworthy. That our leader is unworthy. I would have wrapped her up in the best linen we had on board. Brought her back home, if we are even able to make it back through that mist, but I know Einar would not allow it. He won't risk a chance of disease on such a long trip on the boat. I refused to leave her exposed, though, to be taken by the elements and wild things. She deserves better than the shallow, crude grave I placed her in.

I stand over her grave, unable to mark it. No one will know she is here but me, the wind, and the night sky. They change constantly and move on. So I doubt even they will remember, or that they'll ever come back to visit. I want to lay down, to sleep. The emotional exertion from the night so far has drained me. But the wind shifts again, and a smell of smoke is carried on it, along with distant screams. I stand on my two back legs, sniff the air, and smell fire and blood carried on it.

Looking up towards the village, I can see fires burning much brighter and higher than should be for a normal night. Scanning the beach, I find it empty of any living thing besides myself. Fuck, I had forgotten about them as I tended the girl, pushed them out of my mind. How could I have forgotten about them?! They took advantage of my distraction the moment they saw it consume me and made their silent break towards the village for the mischief and mayhem of the old ways, no doubt led by Anders, that giant fuck who has always schemed for power.

There is no way they didn't notice when I transformed. How stupid of me to clearly demonstrate that all the shit Anders has talked about me to be true to anyone who still needed convincing to go against me. To go against Einar. Proving my incapability, my lack of control. My biggest fear is realized. He was right about me. Shame and embarrassment flood me and I transform back into my human form. Broken, weak both inside and out. Of course, when I need to be the bear, that is when it leaves me. Maybe I am as impotent as Anders says.

The screams continue, and the smoke on the wind grows thicker. I have fucked up the entire mission. Einar will be let down; all my brothers will be let down. Stellan's sacrifice will be for nothing. I have ruined our future. Standing over the Hamingja's grave, I see the would-be home in the future crumbling to dust and ash as I clutch the heart of darkness still around my neck. What would Stellan think?

"He would know you are a failure," the voice of the dead girl whispers in my ear.

Every hair on my body stands up. I look at the spot where I buried her, but the sand is still in place. I look around but see nothing except fires and smoke in the distance.

"But the weight is lifted a little, is it not, once you've accepted the truth?" The voice whispers again. "The anxiety and stress of having to pretend, and the worry about them finding out, which they were always going to eventually, is a little easier to bear. It's time to let out that breath you have been holding since they came for you and Stellan."

She's right of course, the voice. They were always going to find out the truth about me. I've been fighting for so long to hide it from everyone, including myself. To will it to not be. To will a different truth, a different version of myself to come to life. I look up at the burning village, and then back to the sea, out into its vast darkness. I am not meant for Valhalla, but I cannot bear to go to Hel and face all I am indebted to. My only hope would be to be caught in Ran's nets and end up in her kingdom with the drowned.

"Why would the sea god's wife find you worthy enough to catch in her nets? To reside in their kingdom?" the dead girl's voice echoes again, but something seems off about it.

As I spiral into darkness, despair and emptiness, a tiny spark appears inside me. It calls me to save the village. To do something worthy for once, even if it won't pay off my debt or redeem me. Do something! I look at the dark heart stone that Stellan gave me in my hand, and I can almost feel a warmth from it that

I've never felt before. Something inside me urges me to go to the village and lessen the faces that wait for me in Hel. To find my own repayment.

A spark inside me has turned into a fire, and it continues to grow as I turn back to face the village. I start running as fast as I can. No weapons, naked, with only the dark heart of the night now buzzing against my chest as it remains hanging from my neck. I get to where the sand meets the rock barrier and climb, digging my fingers into the craggy spaces in the rock. Nails break and bleed. The smell of smoke and blood overwhelms me as I reach the top of the rocky barrier and ground level of the village. The screams and groans of dying breaths are pounding in my ears.

I pull myself up and am greeted by a dismembered arm lying a few feet in front of me, as if it was carelessly discarded by its butcher. My heart now beats in the same chaotic rhythm as the sounds of violence in front of me. Three gold rings lie around a delicate wrist below curled fingers, with one pointing out. No, not carelessly placed, but purposefully pointing me to the direction of my redemption, showing me the way.

I follow the direction the arm is pointing me in and see more bodies lying outside the first hut on the outskirts of the town. The hut is burning behind them, belongings from inside strewn about. As I continue into the heart of the village, I witness more bodies outside their burning huts. They even slaughtered the animals and set to flame the pens and barns. I can hear the distant booming laughter of Anders up ahead. I pass the first hut towards the village center, each new horror too late for me to stop fills me with anger. I can no longer tell if the burning sensation I feel on my chest is that of my own heart or the dark heart stone.

I continue as fast as I can, passing by the horrors I am moments too late from preventing, when I come to what must have been the village center. Three large poles are already set to flame. While there is no way the others could have set these up, they wasted no time in making use of them. The fires burn so brightly from the pre-kindled pyres, they burn the brightest of anything in the village, casting off an intense heat and light. I finally get near the group of the others, Anders in the middle. Some of the villagers are making a stand, but to no avail. They're quickly dispatched, and the rest are pushed into their huts. I see the doors being tied with rope, and Anders with a torch going over to light another occupied hut. The hamrammr finally hits me, and I am able to transform into my true form in time to knock Anders and another other down with heavy blows from my paws. Anders gets up and starts laughing again, uninjured by my blow.

"Look who finally decided to join the party, boys," he says with a sneer.

The remaining villagers not yet entombed in their burning huts look on in confusion and fear, huddled together like sheep seeking safety in the herd. One tries to make a run for it, but is swiftly taken out by an axe.

"Join us, Bjorn! Prove you're worthy of your gift. Prove it makes you and the other berserkers and Einar better than us. Show us how much Odin is better off having you in his great hall and at his side for the final battle than us!" He nods his crew towards me as he shakes with crazed laughter.

Four of his men come towards me while Anders and a few others turn around to finish their work and move deeper into the village. A spear comes flying and grazes my shoulder, making me release a deafening roar in anger and frustration. We begin to dance the dance of warriors. Moving in and out, shot for shot. Each taking blows and landing shots. The heat of the fire and screams for help intensifies my desperation to make quick work of these men and save who I can.

By the time I have dispatched the four men, it is too late to save those people. I run to catch up with Anders and try to save someone, if anyone is left. The village is large for a fishing village, but it is no match for the surprise attack from Anders and the fourteen others. They worked in deathly teams, quickly and systematically killing everyone and everything in town, swiftly using the initial surprise to their advantage.

I finally catch up to the last group of others at the end of the village by a sea cliff to see Anders and one other warrior kicking down some debris and walking down a path, while the others toy with the last two villagers, drawing out a face-to-face fight with them, whom the men are no match for. The others are entertaining themselves before killing them, like a cat toying with a mouse. I see the men's faces, and one with dark hair whose face is bloodied has a peculiar scent about him; something not quite familiar. The lightly salted scent of his blood temporarily pauses me before I am rudely brought back by a death blow dealt to him and jeering from the small crowd of Anders' men.

Rage fills me once more, and the bear instinct comes out in full force. I charge the others, standing up on hind legs and swatting with my powerful paws, knocking them down and using my teeth and claws to tear flesh and break bones. Blood mattes my fur and flows freely in and out of my mouth. I feel a searing pain as one of the warriors manages to strike me with their sword, slicing into my hind. I roar in fury, moving to swat them, but am hindered by the pain and weakness caused by the strike. We fight, and eventually I am able

to overtake them all, but not in time to save the two
men.

IONNA

THE SELKIE BEACH

17

MOTHER, GRANT US THE SAFETY OF YOUR WATERS

The boys stand huddled together, their bodies as still as statues, gripping each other's hands tightly. A few of the Selkies in human form cross the boundary where the sand and sea meet. I do not have time to process the magnitude of the Selkie crossing. After everything that happened back at the hut with Daithí and Cian, I am relieved to see my true family has not abandoned me. The flames of determination that had replaced the emptiness from the fallout are now joined with hope.

The boys do not fight as each one is scooped into an unknown relative's arms, except to maintain their grip on each other, which is unwillingly broken. They are unaware it will be the last time they ever cross that boundary themselves. I give my daughter to Aine as she cries out for me.

"It's okay, Naia. You know me, sweet child," Aine says, trying to soothe her, petting her hair and looking her in the eyes as she wraps my skin tighter around my child.

"Her coat, it's not finished." she says, her eyes growing even larger as she grabs the unfinished sleeve on Naia's little arm.

"I know." I say quickly, cutting my hand with Daithí's whalebone knife and running into the surf to cut one hand of each boy.

"I'm sorry, I'm sorry." I say as they both cry out. "It's going to be okay. You're going home with my family now. With your Sea family." I lay a hand and plant a kiss on each boy's head before cutting their hands.

I join my hand with my Caden's and kiss him one last time before letting him go with one of my brothers into the Sea. I do the same for our youngest son.

"Momma!" Aidan calls out for the last time.

One of his arms is wrapped around the neck of the Selkie who carries him, and the other reaches for me. I can see the fear on his face as I watch them both disappear beneath the waves, along with the song from my family, who carries them. I didn't have time to sing to them before they were carried under. I pray my family's song will be enough.

Please work, I beg silently.

I run back to my daughter, taking her from Aine's arms and dressing her in the unfinished coat as Aine tries to talk to me. I can't focus on her words as I try to finish sewing what I can of Naia's sleeve. My fingers on my cut hand go numb and make it harder to hold on to the needle. Both of us are crying now, both in fear. Her also in confusion. I don't have time to explain to her, to make her understand what's going on, why I'm being scary, why our whole world at this moment is scary. She clings to me in desperation. I try to pull her arms back so I can finish sewing.

"Aine, please." I yell in frustration, gesturing towards Naia as I try to work around her arms and body that grasp me.

I am struggling to provide to her what I gave her brothers, and I know that I am failing.

"Please work!" I beg, no longer silently, but crying out the words in frustration, anger and fear. "Please work for me, for once."

She was the one I was most sure the coat would work on. I had saved hers for last because I was so sure. Now it looks like I have doomed her with my certainty. I had left my baby for last, never thinking I wouldn't finish in time. It is such a small coat, and I underestimated the time needed to complete it, failing her.

Booming laughter interrupts my hurried work as it's carried down the beach by the wind. Large men, unlike any I have seen before are coming down the same path the children and I had fled from. Their beards and bodies are covered in what I assume to be blood and ash, based on the screams from the village above that have grown quieter and the visible large fires still rising from the huts. I know in this moment that those in the village will all be dead soon. My daughter and I will likely be too, if this does not work.

How many times can a heart break in one night? How many times can the thundering echo of pain, fear and anger still build up inside me like waves that crest and then fall only to build and crest again. From my knees I scream as my daughter clings to Aine, sobbing so hard she is visibly shaking.

"Ionna, enough!" Aine roars as she rips my daughter's arm out of my hands and pulls her away from me.

The white bone needle swings from the thread of the dark unfinished sleeve of her coat as Aine rushes into the surf. I sit there, still kneeling in the wet sand unable to move. I hear her let out a high-pitched scream followed by hysterical crying and look over to see that Aine has done what I could not. She runs back, as if forgetting the second part and now urgently presses Naia's bleeding hand hard into mine.

"Thank you." I manage to choke out.

After letting our blood combine for a brief moment, she turns around with my daughter and rushes back to the Sea. I hear her feet enter the water. I feel something rush past my face, and hear the Seals start barking loudly again in panic. I feel in my head the same pain every Selkie is left feeling, a painful searing pain in their heads. The pain that comes from the death of the matriarch. I turn around to see Aine collapse into the water through eyes still fuzzy from the intense pain in my head. I stumble forward, pushing through the agony as my daughter drops from her hands and Aine's body falls limp, a large spear sticking out of her back.

I find the strength to get up and run over to them. I struggle to pull her coat off through the spear and off her body. When I finally manage to free her skin, I wrap it around my daughter over the unfinished coat I made her. The horror of what I'm doing pales in comparison to the horror I feel when I look to see the men still coming towards us, staring in amusement. Their laughter is carried down by the wind.

I pick up my daughter now wrapped up twice and wade out into the shallow waves as fast as I can, struggling to not fall in my haste. I try to choke out words, prayers, pleas for mercy, and forgiveness through my tears, but nothing is happening. I look back towards the beach, keeping my back turned to the men who are now almost upon us. I drop my knees and cradle my daughter into my chest as the water covers us up to my shoulders, leaving both our heads just above it. It's not working. It's not working. I look desperately out towards the open for my sisters and brothers who have all fled to the safety of deeper water.

I am alone.

I have no other options to save my daughter. I have failed. I have failed my daughter I have failed my husband. I have failed her father. I have failed as a mother, both human and Selkie. And I have failed as a sister.

The waves knock my sister's body into us, pushing both our faces briefly under. I struggle against my wet dress that wraps around my legs like a rope to stand up. I see the spear still sticking out of Aine's body. I know my only options now are to grab my daughter and try to swim out into the sea or to fight. If I try to swim, I will drown us both trying to keep us afloat in this form, weighed down by these clothes. We will likely be hit with a spear in the back like my sister as we try to flee. I see no other option. I must fight.

I turn, walk back to shallower water, and put my daughter down as she grabs my leg from behind. I place my other leg on my sisters' body and hold her down so I can find the strength to pull out the spear. Picking up my daughter with one hand, I turn back around to face the men with the weapon in my other.

I welcome all the emotions that come flooding back to me and draw upon them for strength. They swirl inside me like a whirlpool, growing and sucking everything inside of it. Everything I have felt since my childhood, since I left the water. The unfairness of what followed in the village, at the loss of my child to the woods. At the betrayal from my husband and my lover. The feeling of seeing my family willingly cross the barrier and welcoming my children back home with them. The feeling of failing my daughter and myself.

I use these emotions and let them fuel the dark desire that has been inside me since childhood. The one that called to me to wander, to go to places that were not meant for me. The one that caused the accident that marked my sister. I let it brew and stew and as I face these men, I let it feed my anger. For too long I have let myself be influenced and carried off in any direction the wind of misfortune and humans blew. No longer. The human winds can blow all they want, but I will not be carried by them any longer.

We may die, but I will die fighting. I grip my spear and daughter tighter, lowering the spear in a defensive position. I let out a loud, shrill bark that causes the men to laugh again. But I don't care. The opinions of men hold no sway over me anymore. I have lived the human life for too long. No longer pushing away the Sea, I will die a Selkie.

EINAR

THE WOODS

18

THE WASHERWOMAN

"What do I need to create the new world, a new land for me and my people?" I ask, still holding firmly onto her.

"Your light, your luck, has already run out. But then, that was never your luck or light, was it?" she asks.

The washer woman continues to slosh in the water, taking out clothing and moving to beat it against the bank beside her, unbothered and unencumbered by my grip on her long, snake-like breast. The cloth is stained red with blood as she untwists it and lays it flat to dry before moving on to the next piece in the water. From the side I can see the true horror of her nature. A gaping mouth, exposed teeth and jaw blackened with death and rot.

"No," I respond back. "It was—"

Suddenly, I hear the screams of my men. It breaks the quietness of the moment between me and the crone. I look back at the woman and recognize the piece of clothing she untwists as belonging to Iver. I can see the rips and blood stains in it as she lays it flat before beginning again to work on the next piece of her washing. They need me, but I am so close now. I can't stop. I am moments away from getting the answers I need. I need the men to not fail me, I need them to hold on a minute longer.

"Tell me what I need." I demand of her.

"Tsk, tsk, child, isn't it obvious? You know in your heart what you need. You know in your heart what you lack. What you've always lacked," she says, continuing her chore.

"Einar!" I hear Olaf cry out.

The screams and sounds of violence continue behind me as she cackles again.

"Tell me!" I yell, pulling on her breast hard and squeezing painful. She laughs as if I'm nothing more than a young child throwing a tantrum.

"You need what you took for your own, used as your own, but was not truly yours."

"The only luck you can count on..." she continues.

"Is the luck you make yourself; you earn yourself." I say, finishing her sentences as she untwists and lays out the next piece of bloodied clothing belonging to another one of my men.

I look at the clothes lining on the banks of the river and notice tunics and pieces I recognize as belonging to the others who I left with Bjorn. She reaches for another piece of clothing as I think about my next question. A hand grabs my shoulder in desperation.

"Einar, we have to go, Brothers are dying and..." Gunnar stops mid-sentence, and I can see his eyes have fallen upon the line of familiar clothing.

Gunnar, with his dirty blonde hair covered in blood becomes a sheet of white under the grime of battle, piecing together the washer woman's work and what's happening behind us.

"Einar, make her stop," he pleads, pointing at my hand that is still connected to her.

"Isn't there something more you'd like to know?" The washerwoman asks, her hand still fishing in the water for another piece of clothing.

"Einar!" Olaf yells again.

"Einar, make her stop or I will!" Gunnar says, raising his sword and moving forward to strike at her.

"Stop now, no more washing," I command her.

She lets out a heavy sigh but complies. Standing up and walking into the water, she fades with each step.

Gunnar turns to run back, and I follow him to the ruined manor. Iver is on the ground, bleeding, and a small, squat creature who resembles an old man fills what looks like a red hat with Iver's blood. I pick up my sword, frustrated at having to end my conversation with the washerwoman early, and swing it at the creature as it jumps back just in time.

I yell to the others to run as I continue to swing my sword in anger at the old goblin. Iver is too far gone, and I yell at the others to leave him as we race back to the bridge. I'm relieved to see Leif still there, but something is wrong; he is no longer in bear form, and I see he is crouched over Mads, who is holding his side.

I yell at them as we run and jump one by one over the crumbling bridge. I start kicking the stones and stomping to make the bridge finish crumbling, though the red blood-capped goblin appears to not have given chase past its lair.

"We need to go, now," I say.

Leif helps Mads up, and no one argues with me as I start running back down the path towards the beach. The line of clothing I saw from the old crone worries me that we may be too late already, and I worry that Bjorn has finally lost it.

Ionna

The Selkie Beach

19

— · —

A SELKIE'S LAST STAND

I can see them sneering in amusement, their ugly, bearded faces laughing in entertainment. Their heavy-framed bodies, strange clothes of light leather armor and long, braided hair paint a grotesque image of who these strangers are. We are game to them, and this is just another hunt for these killers. Rage and defiance still course through my veins, even as I struggle to keep my spear raised. The numbness from the cut in my hand is now moving up into my arm, fighting against my will to not give up. As they get closer, I can smell the disgusting scent of old grease, smoke, and blood. I know we will die.

"Naia, if mommy falls down, you run as fast and deep as you can into the water," I say.

Her little hands grip my leg tighter in response. There is still a chance it could work, though. She wears two coats, her blood has mixed with both mine and Aine's in the water. As the whirlpool continues to swirl inside me, gaining strength and speed, the defiant voice inside me grows.

I will not go down easily. I will give Naia as much time for the coats and magic to work as I can. Before the men can get any closer, a deafening roar is let out from something behind them. The men had no time to react, to scream. They are now lifeless bodies covered in blood on the ground. Their mauled bodies lie on the sand not twenty yards from us, and a great russet bear covered in scars and blood and ash is standing where they once stood not moments ago. It is shaking in fury, covered in the men's blood.

Bears have always been natural enemies of Seals; I should feel terror. Instead, I feel a small sense of relief. They have hunted us for as long as we have both existed. But if I am to die, I would rather it be by beast than man. Either way, I still fight for my daughter. I stare the beast down in his eyes and tighten my grip on the spear. The great bear lets out another terrible roar, making my stomach drop, but I steady myself.

"Come on." I mutter.

Impatiently, I wait for its charge. I am left to wait longer as it drops down on to all fours but does not move towards us.

"Come on!" I scream at the bear, gripping my spear.

It pants heavily instead of charging. It sniffs the air towards us, perhaps realizing we are the same as its favorite prey. As it stands on its two back legs to sniff higher in the air, I think this is it, the moment it will charge, and get ready for its attack. I keep the spear lowered so when it charges, I can do my best to use its own force against it. If it doesn't knock the spear out of my hands first, we may have a chance to survive. Time seems to move slowly as I wait and anticipate the beast's next move. I make peace with my death, and that I did all I could to save my children this time. But I will not give up on Naia.

"Naia, you are a Selkie like mommy. We are strong, and we are fierce. We are of the water. I need you to start walking into the Sea. It will take you like it did your brothers and your Sea family. I need you to trust the water, to trust mommy."

I begin to sing my grandmother's song. Quietly at first, then louder, stronger, letting the wind carry my voice to the Sea. The bear lowers back onto all fours and walks towards us, slowly, sniffing the air. I sing louder, yelling the words to the song of the devil on the land, the devil on the sea, and the one who captured me.

The great bear turns suddenly and places his back to us. I stop singing, surprised and confused. I look past him to see what he is focused on, and see that the bear now stands between us and more men coming down the path. These men are much larger than the ones who now lay in torn heaps on the ground. Larger than any human I have ever seen before. It once again stands and lets out a roar before dropping back down and pacing back and forth in front of us protectively, unwilling to share its catch.

I thank the Sea for the opportunity the diversion of the men has presented. Picking Naia up in my one arm, I start to back slowly into the Sea. I take a deep breath in, preparing to sing once more when a shift in the wind brings a surprise to me. The men's smell, it's not the same as the men before them. Not the same as the men of the village. It is also not the same as ours. These men, their smell is not completely animal and not completely human.

As the men get closer, I hear the smallest one say over the breeze, "Easy now brother, we've just come from the woods to find this. We saw what happened in the village to the villagers, and to our brothers. Calm yourself, change back and let us speak."

The bear again lets out a deafening roar, then turns its great head back towards me and my daughter, and I feel as though there is a hint of something familiar in its eyes. I take another step back, silently as Naia clings to me and buries her face in my wet tangled hair as the bear and I continue to lock eyes. The bear breaks our gaze and lets out a guttural groan turning back around and changing into the form of a large, naked man. He is one of them, the men who slaughtered the village. But he is also like us, in that he is not a human. He is of both worlds, like we are.

BJORN

THE SELKIE BEACH

20

ANOTHER DEBT OWED

Her long, dark hair is wet and clings to her pale face and body. Her dark eyes stare wide at me. In one arm, she carries a small child, dark and pale as her mother. In the other arm she holds a spear pointed right at me. She is as still as a statue. She smells strongly of the sea, the blood dripping from her cut hand just as salty as the water around her. I take a hobbled step forward and rise in pain to stand on my back legs. She meets me and my movement by lowering the spear, as if to end my life should I charge.

Suddenly she begins to sing, quietly at first, and then louder. Her words hit me, and I understand now that this woman is not a villager. She doesn't smell or look anything like the bodies I ran across and failed to save. She is of the sea. She is Rán. The little one must be one of her seven daughters, Bára perhaps.

The only good death I could ever picture for myself is finally here. I feel light in my heart for the first time, and love. I lumber with my ruined leg over to them and get closer. She holds steady with her spear. Strange how she doesn't carry a net. I raise my muzzle up again to sniff the air and catch their scent and am hit with the scent of my brothers and Einar. I unwillingly turn away from Rán and her little Bára to face the intrusion of my brothers. If I tried to go with her now, they would surely stop me. I need to find a way to get them away from her, so she will take me with them.

"Easy now brother, we've just come from the woods to find this. We saw what happened in the village to the villagers, and to our brothers. Calm yourself, change back and let us speak," Einar says.

EINAR

THE SELKIE BEACH

21

LUCK THAT IS OUR OWN

I knew when I saw the old hag wring out the blood-tinted water from the battle-stained tunics of the men who had traveled with us on this mission that I had lost him.

I wasn't sure how far, or if I would even find him alive. Find any of them alive. Seeing the carnage from the village, on the trail of death we followed, I can tell there had been two separate massacres this night. I already know which one he was responsible for.

Coming down the path, I see his russet fur matted down and stained with blood and soot. I call out to him and can see that he is injured as he turns around and transforms back into his human form. Walking towards us, I can see from his gait how badly his leg has been injured. There is something different about his eyes now that surprises me. They are not the big, sad eyes he had when I last left him. Nor the frenzied eyes he wears during battle. They are alight with something new. He no longer seems on the edge of losing himself, no. There is a confidence in him that I have never witnessed before, despite his seemingly broken body.

"Brother," he says as he nears me.

I reach out and grab his arm, pulling him into an embrace. Looking past his shoulder out towards the sea, I see a frail woman in the surf holding a spear in one hand and a bundle of something in the other. The washerwoman had said I would find what I needed on the beach, but I can't imagine anything here would help me. Not in this state, anyways.

"You're alive!" Mads' voice cuts through, and I let go of my embrace on Bjorn so Mads can access him.

"I am, Brother."

Mads winces in Bjorn's embrace.

Pulling back from Bjorn's arms, Mads says, "You look like shit."

Bjorn smiles.

I turn my back away from the woman with the spear and look to see what remains of my two top men on this mission. We took many losses in the woods, even more in this village. A simple fucking task I had given him. Though I am relieved to see he is still alive, he is ruined as a warrior. Not only has he ruined himself, but from what we saw in the village and the bloody mess on this beach, he also took out every single warrior who was not in the woods with me.

"Bjorn," I say, interrupting his reunion with Mads.

He looks up at me, eyes still alight with something that puts a sense of uneasiness with me. Though injured, he is still quite larger than me, unpredictable. I can't help but feel as though he is not completely under my command anymore. No longer sad and needy, there is a calmness that wasn't there before. At least, not unless Stellan was around. His blood brother Stellan is still under my control, and if we can get out of here, I may have to use him to bring Bjorn back to heel or out of the way.

"Bjorn, you were supposed to keep the men away from this village."

My words, the disapproval in my voice, they do nothing to him. His eyes do not avert, his shoulders do not slump. I feel a small flutter rise in the bottom of my stomach, and I work to push it down. I am still in control here; I will bring him back to heel. He looks at me in silence, still holding on to Mads in a half embrace while Mads leans into him for support, one hand laying against the wound on his side. His eyes meeting mine.

"You," I say gesturing at him and Mads, "them," I say, pointing at the broken bodies of what was Anders and Sven, then, raising my arm, I point up the village saying, "a failure."

He continues to look at me, but his eyes now change to look hard, and I can see Mads leaning into him to say something.

"We needed them to get us back off the island. We needed..."

"No, you needed brothers, Einar," he says, pulling away from his half embrace with Mads and taking a bold step forward towards me.

He postures himself in an offensive position that, despite his clearly damaged leg, still feels threatening. A challenge no brother has dared give me since our early years; not since the time of my father, when such insubordination would be dealt with swiftly and painfully. I struggle to hide my shock and confusion as to what the fuck is going on here. He has completely lost his mind to challenge me like this.

"All you needed was Brothers. Your job was to get them in and out of the woods. Yet," he pauses, raising his hands to point to the small fraction of the brothers who made it out of the woods with me, "they are missing. Where are they?!"

No, demands. As if he is the one in control. My anger starts to build, the shock fading into the background. Bjorn has never been in control, yet here he is, trying to challenge me and mine.

"They are lost because they did not follow my fucking orders!"

Pointing at Mads I continue, "This one is injured because he ran off like your weaker brothers."

Standing up to posture the same as Bjorn, though he winces from the bleeding wound on his side, Mads calmly says, "They are gone because of your poor leadership. Because you lost sight and lost control. This goes against the promise you made to us. They need to be recovered."

"No, we cannot afford to lose any more men. We don't have enough to properly man the ship back as it is," I say, staring Mads down.

What was it Father had said? 'It only takes one to step out of line and weaken your chain on them.'

"We will look in the village for survivors and use them to fill the gaps." Mads says, not backing down despite the heat he must be feeling from my disapproval.

"No, we would have seen them had there been any, and the ones who may yet still be alive will be dead soon or are too wounded to be of use," I say.

"They may have fled into the woods, same as the boy. We can—"

"I said no."

"What is the fucking point then? Why did you bring us here? How is this world of yours any better than what we left? Please remind me, because this seems like more of the same. More of your father. I still believe in a better way of being. I am staying. To look for survivors, to find the missing child and to give the dead a proper burial. To right the wrong of Einar for putting trust in wolves instead of bears," Mads rages at me.

"For putting his trust in a demon hag for answers while our brothers died," Gunnar's voice suddenly chimes in.

He is the youngest of the brothers, and the last one I expected to speak out or betray me. His young face looks troubled beneath the mess of yellow hair stained with blood. Mads, Bjorn, and now Gunnar all stare at me, and I know that there is a fracture in the group that I cannot ignore and must deal with soon before it grows.

"My will is not for any of you to question. You have followed me this far, men. You have seen what I am capable of, what I have accomplished so far. You have seen what I am willing to sacrifice for you. I have never failed you. Do not threaten me, and do not forget who I am and what I have done for you all," I say, seething with anger and working hard to remain in control of it.

I look back at the woman in the sea as Bjorn turns his back on me and makes his way back to her slowly with his injured leg. I can now see the bundle of clothing she holds contains a child, a girl. Suddenly it all makes sense—the washerwoman's words, the words of the

Volva. Luck that is my own, luck that I can make. Luck in a child who I can mold into the vision I can see so clearly now.

Unlike father's failed attempt to mold me. Unlike his failed attempts to mold the brothers into warriors with unwavering allegiance. Gunnar was the youngest brother to come to the pits at six. His betrayal proves that he was already too old to be fully molded. This child looks to be much younger than he was then. I am certain I will be successful with it. The washerwoman said as much.

"Fine, Mads," I say, turning back to face him and Gunnar.

"We will take any survivors we can find in a quick sweep, but we leave the dead and gravely wounded. And no one enters the woods," I speak loud enough for all the brothers to hear.

I can hear Holger grumbling, and I know that at least some brothers still remain true to me. The sun rises over the sea and beach, creating a warm glow that surrounds the little girl, a sure sign of what she is destined to be. I can feel the pull of my success pushing me on, it won't be long now. The new world awaits, and she is the vessel to carry me to it.

Ionna

The Selkie Beach

22

THE TIES THAT BIND US

The russet bear man and the second group of war-riors now stand together under the rising sun and setting moon, which the pale sand of the cold beach lies under. The distant wall of thick mist on top of the ocean behind me is becoming more visible as the sun continues its journey to rise higher than the moon.

The whirling pool of emotion that was swirling dangerously inside me has begun to slow down. Though my body is still carrying the tension and sensitivity of being on high alert, exhaustion starts creeping in around the edges of my bones and spirit. I am not sure how they managed to get through it, or what their intent to get back, if they plan to leave at all, will be.

What was it Aine had said all those weeks ago? That they had carried a light with them able to penetrate the mist? Looking at the group of bloodied and burly men, I see no light beyond that from the rising sun.

The light that danced in the sky last night had quickly dispersed. If that is what got them through, it seems as though it will no longer be here to see them back through, unless they carry more of it with them.

I continue to clutch on to Naia with failing strength from the loss of blood and effort of surviving the night that is finally ending. I am not sure what the day will bring, but I know I am on borrowed time.

Reaching my lips down to plant them on top of her head that is damp from the spray of the Sea on the wind as I tighten my arm tighter around her with conjured strength. I know I am done giving up. I am done with defeat. We are both soaked to the bone, but she seems as unbothered by the cold as I am. The double layer of mine and my sister's skin provide her some comfort against the cold and harsh elements of the night and morning. She is barely visible amongst the bundle of leather except for her tiny pale face peeking out with large, dark eyes.

Keeping an eye on the men on the beach a few yards ahead of me I continue slowly backing into the water. I hum a song that is my own. A song to the Sea that asks for forgiveness and acceptance. That asks for the safe passage of my daughter. I sing the words of the song that I have written in my heart and blood. I sing the words that asks the Sea to once again flow through my veins and soul. To fill me with all the parts of it that I had rejected for all these years.

Naia, exhausted, looks up with eyes filled with both curiosity and caution before laying her tired head back down on my shoulder, surrendering to the lullaby I have made for us and the Sea. I never realized what a brave and steady little girl she was. She has overcome the nightmare of last night and the pain and confusion that it brought. I look at her and am amazed at the strength within her that I never noticed before, at the trust she puts in me, a trust I didn't even think I had in me. With every growing inch of water that we become submerged in, my confidence grows, and I think I can start to feel a faint tingle in my skin.

I look back to see the russet haired bear man locking my eyes once again. He starts to run towards us, bursting back into bear form as he rushes the water. I step quicker into deeper water until the waves are at my chest and only our heads are above the waves. It's going to work; I know it's going to work. The tingling in my skin grows stronger as I move to pull Naia's arms from around my neck and take us both under, I am suddenly grabbed by two large strong hands around my waist that pulls us swiftly back up and out.

"No!" I yell in rage, one hand around Naia and one reaching for the water.

I see my family bobbing out in the water silently, no more help coming from them.

With damp sand under my feet, once again anchored to the land, I lash out in rage against the strong large hands that had caught us like a fishing net and hauled us back. I let go of Naia and turn on the now-human body that belonged to the nets. Hitting and scratching with my hands and fists at the body as hard and unmoving as a seaside mountain. I howl and hit like a violent wind trying to tear it down. I scream until I hear Naia cry out in fear. I freeze, my hands still on the chest of the beast that breathes in steadily. I feel his heart beating in a fast rhythm under my sore fists.

Something about the way he breathes in and out feels familiar. Like his breath is in rhythm with the waves. Like Daithí's was. Daithí, who I loved, but should have never trusted. I look up and meet his almond shaped eyes, which are the color of honey. There is a warmth I feel, or am imagining, coming from them, asking me to trust them, but I reject it. I am done trusting anything from the land. I trusted Daithí and it led to betrayal.

I drop my hands back to my sides and turn my head to look back at Naia who huddles, frightened in the layers of seal skin. I look back up again at the bear man, with his russet hair and beard and I turn my back on him to walk back to my daughter. Picking her up, I turn back to him saying, "What do you want?'

"Please, take me with you," he says, dropping to his knees.

"What?"

"Please Rán, cast your net around me and take me with you and little Bára. I beg you," he says, pleading with me.

"I am Ionna, and this is Naia. We can't take you with us; you are not of the Sea," I reply.

I do not know who these people are he has confused us for, but maybe he will let us go once he realizes we are not who he thinks. That we cannot take him with us.

"Now let us go," I say, commanding, as if I am a matriarch.

Ionna

The Selkie Beach

23

THE CHOICES WE MAKE

"Bjorn!" The small, dark-haired man calls, with a large injured red-haired man and another with brown hair coming towards us with him.

The russet-haired bear man still kneeling before me does not answer them, he continues to look at me and Naia as if waiting for us to do something. His eyes finally look away, defeated as he stands up after a few moments of silence.

"You saw I protected you from those men last night," he says in a quiet voice, speaking to us for the first time since I denied his request to accompany us into the Sea. His voice is low, and softer than I expected it to be.

"I promise I will continue to protect you. I am called Bjorn. I assume you can sense that I am not the same as the men who attacked you, as I can sense that you are also not the same as the people in the village."

"You look like them," I retort back. "You look like those same men to me. You look human."

"As do you and your daughter look human to us," he replies, raising his hand toward me, as if expecting me to take it.

I stand my ground and do not step back or flinch as I refuse his hand. The men continue walking towards us, getting closer to where we are. Why did I not play into his desperation to flee with us? It occurs to me too late that I could have pretended and let him follow us to drown or swim back. Either way, we would have been free, and I am angry at myself for thinking of it too late.

"We both know looks can be deceiving," he says, keeping his hand outstretched.

I see the man smile as I feel Naia leaning forward in my arms towards the man, her tiny arm outstretched towards his.

"No," I tell her sharply, pushing her arm back down.

"Look Bjorn, someone actually likes you," the red-haired man, the largest of all the men in the group, says in an amused voice as they close in around us.

I continue to stand my ground, despite the growing number surrounding me. The waves lap at my feet, pulling the bottom of my dress against my legs, my feet sinking a little deeper into the sand with each round of the waters pull, as if now begging me to come back further into it. Twice now we have been denied access to the sanctuary of the water, so I ignore its hands around my ankles and stand firmly where I am.

I can smell the blood weeping from the wound the red-haired man covers with his hand on his bare stomach. It smells the same as Bjorn's, who remains facing us, a faint smile briefly materializing before disappearing just as quickly across his face.

Bjorn brings his outstretched arm down and stands tall amongst the group of men. He is the second largest next to the red-haired man, though they seem to carry the most wounds between them out of the group. The men are naked except for two of them.

The smaller, dark-haired one with eyes so bright and blue that they look unnatural has a scent that is muted compared to the others. Like Naia, he is not quite a human, and not quite a bear. The other man still clothed is a bear, the same as the rest. I am not sure why he remains clothed, other than he must not have changed into his true form last night. Both of their clothing carries the stains of death and violence. The blood they wear is unlike anything I have sensed before, though; some of it is human, but some of it is different, and I can't place what the scent belongs to. The men stand in front of me but make no move to go beyond the water's edge.

We sit in what feels like a long silence when the dark-haired man with the piercing blue eyes speaks.

"I am Einar," the man says, his expression matching the calm and authoritative nature of his voice. "I apologize for what happened to your people, to your village. I want you to know it was not on my orders. My men and I, we have only come here in search of something to help us build a better world. One where violence like what has befallen your village becomes only an old, unpleasant memory," he continues.

The weight of his eyes feels sharp, like the end of a hook waiting for me to bite at the bait of his words. It's uncomfortable, his gaze, but I refuse to look away, to show weakness. I meet it until I notice him look away for a brief second at my daughter before returning it to me. I swear I saw a small change in his eyes as they moved to my daughter, but it was brief, and his eyes have returned to being calm and unrevealing.

I can feel all their stares, searching me, looking for anything I might give up. They will not find weakness here; that part of me has died a million times over the night. The other man who is dressed steps forward, sniffing in the air like the animal he holds inside him.

"She is not one of them." The man says, taking another step forward.

He continues towards me until Bjorn's arm shoots out and stops him, creating a barrier between us and them.

"Who's to say she isn't," Bjorn says his face hardening.

"Let the woman tell us for herself before we all choke on the smell of your crusty old ass. Seriously, when was the last time you took a bath, Holger?" The red-haired man says, wincing in pain and forcing a smile.

Einar nods his head in agreement, saying, "So be it, Mads. But watch your tongue in front of the woman and child."

"Please, given what's happened to the poor child, I'm sure my tongue is of the least concern. Besides, it was funny!"

Holger's face hardens, and he lets out a low growl between clenched teeth. A slight movement of Einar's thick brow betrays an annoyance at Mads.

"Well then, tell us in your own words," Einar says to me.

They all stare at me, waiting once more, and I fight the urge to shift my weight or move at all in case they read it as a sign for weakness or opportunity.

"I am, and I am not. As you are and are not," I say with as much confidence as I can muster, letting them know I can read them as easily as they can read me.

"That is seal skin the child wears," Holger says, raising his hand to point to Naia who continues to remain quiet. He does not pass beyond the still outstretched arm of Bjorn. I cannot tell if it is out of fear or respect. If Bjorn outranks him in whatever hierarchy, they have.

"So it is," Einar says, as if considering something, once again looking at Naia in a way that makes me uncomfortable.

"The same color as the seals we saw when coming through the mist." Holger continues.

Einar stands, still looking at Naia and I resist the urge to pull her away and hide her. I must remain strong though and not show any sign of weakness.

"Why did you and your child not flee into the water as the others did? And where is that one's coat?" Holger continues his line of questioning, pointing at Aine's naked, dead body that still lies in the surf.

I say nothing.

"That skin looks much larger than what a child as small as that would need. If you skin a bear, the skin is sized to fit the bear, surely seal skins are the same," he continues.

"Enough," Bjorn growls, turning on the men and once again placing himself between us and them. I feel a small amount of gratitude towards him for not saying that he pulled us out of the water.

I am surprised they did not witness it the way he came running down towards us. They seem too focused on our skin, and I am not sure for what purpose. I continue to remain silent, not confirming nor denying about our skin and relationship to the water. I know they can sense our blood, but I do not think it is wise to betray our secrets yet. Though Holger has all but guessed it.

"Stand aside, Bjorn, Holger asks fair questions. We need the answers to help this woman and her child," Einar says.

"He said enough." Mads says, moving to stand beside Bjorn.

I can see Einar's face, still wearing the same calm expression that securely keeps the truth of his thoughts hidden. His eyes are still focused on Naia, and she retreats into the layers of seal skin like a turtle hiding safely in its shell. I feel slightly better having Mads and Bjorn forming a protective wall against Einar and Holger as the rest of the men remain watching and waiting further up the beach. Their size is impressive, even amongst the grouping of men who are by far much larger than the men from the village had been. Than Cian and Daithí had been. They are both carrying wounds, though, Bjorn's leg and Mads' side. I don't know if they could overpower Einar and Holger, who appear to be without injuries, though they are smaller.

"Enough," Einar says seemingly having a change of heart.

"Mads, you have work to do in the village, and a child in the woods to find."

A child in the woods? For the first time since I let all the emotions swirl inside me and made my stance, another shock wave hits me. Einar must have picked up on the changes inside me. Cian always said I wore my emotions on my face.

"Are you missing a child?" Einar questions me, eyebrows raising in what would be a convincing display of concern if it wasn't coming from a man leading a group of mostly naked warriors covered in blood.

I look up at him, trying to keep my face from betraying me, but I can feel my eyes widen.

"It wasn't a human child," Holger adds, a small smirk crossing his face as he nods towards Naia.

"The fuck would you know, Holger, you ugly shit. Your nose has been broken so many times it can't smell the difference between my sweaty balls and a piece of freshly baked honey bread," Mads jumps in, looking back and giving me a small shake of his head as if he knows the question inside me.

"Fuck off, Mads," Holger spits as he takes an aggressive step forward but is stopped by Einar's hand on his shoulder. His face contorts in a way that increases his troll-like features.

Einar, with a calm face, always calm. Too calm, like the surface of the water under a rip current as it pulls you out to drown.

"I have asked Mads to lead the search effort for survivors in the village."

"The fuck you did," Mads interjects.

Einar, unshaken by Mads, continues, "To include a small boy we encountered in the woods. You are welcome to join him. We can get you and your child off the beach. We'll place the child on our boat for safety while you join Mads to search." He begins to take a step forward towards Naia but stops when I take a step closer to Bjorn.

"No." I say firmly, shaking my head.

A small part of me is screaming yes, trying to be heard. He had said small child. Not a human child. Cael wouldn't be a small child anymore. *He couldn't possibly still be the same, frozen in time from when I lost him, could he? There is magic in the woods. What if?*

That small voice inside me cries out again. It wasn't but hours ago that I had been determined to go to the woods to find him. But now, with these strange men giving me the option, mentioning a small child seems too good to be true. What was it the villagers had believed? That the creatures in the woods would send back one of their own in the skin of your loved one as a replacement? I look down at Naia.

"*How do you choose,*" I had asked Aine.

"*I don't know,*" she had said, "*you do the best you can, knowing it may not be the right choice.*"

Turning from Naia's face to the Sea before looking back down at her, I know. I must choose the one who needs me the most right now. Caden and Aidan are safely in the Sea with my family. Cael is gone. He has been for so long. I am not giving up on him, but Naia needs me the most right now.

I am sorry, I think to him. I will come back for you one day; I renew my promise. Right now, I need to focus on Naia.

I look back at the four men in front of me.

"No." I say again.

"Then no it is," Einar replies. "Mads, you are free to start your search in the village and woods, but we are leaving soon. If you are not back by the time the boat is loaded and ready to go, then we leave without you. What is your name?" Einar asks, turning back to look at me. But I say nothing.

"You and the child are to come with us. There is nothing left here for you but death and destruction. We will bring you back to our home, where you can start anew, where you will be safe," Einar says, unfazed by my silence.

Though his words are meant to comfort and entice me, they do the opposite.

"No," I say.

"I wasn't asking," Einar says.

"She said no," Bjorn says in a low voice.

"He wasn't asking," Holger jumps back in, reaching for my arm, which Bjorn quickly blocks again, and the two men begin to posture against one another.

"Holger, step aside. Bjorn, look at the village, look at what you let happen. We have been through the woods and back, we know the dangers that are in there, and we know what will be drawn with the scent of the massacre. Do you really want to leave this poor woman and her child to that?"

Bjorn stands quietly, as if considering his words.

"I don't think you want to be responsible for their deaths, too," Einar says. "You are responsible, though. Make sure you get them safely to the boat and settled in for the trip."

Einar taps Holger on his shoulder, signaling to his guard dog to head back up to the beach with him, where the rest of the men are waiting. I stand here with Naia, Mads and Bjorn with their backs to us, still standing guard in front.

"You don't have to go with them," Mads says to Bjorn before turning to face me and saying, "Neither do you."

Bjorn doesn't say anything.

"I am not going back," Mads says. "I wouldn't make the trip, anyways." We can stay here together, the four of us. Look for survivors, help rebuild, maybe."

Bjorn looks at me, then back at Mads.

"There is nothing to rebuild, Anders and the others made sure of that. They slaughtered everything, even the animals. Einar is right, I am responsible. For the village, and for them." He turns to look at me.

"I will protect you both. I know of someplace safe once we make it back to our homeland. I can help you both get to safety and start anew. Whether that is settling with us or finding a way back to your kind," he says, pointing out to the sea.

Turning back to Mads, Bjorn removes a black stone necklace that he had been wearing and places it around Mads' neck.

"Bjorn, no." Mads chokes. The large, strong man before me begins to soften, and tears well in his eyes.

"I should have given this to you earlier on the beach, but I was much weaker then," Bjorn says, placing a hand on each of Mads' biceps as they stand facing each other, the necklace now hanging around Mads' neck.

"I am sorry brother. I am sorry I wasn't with you in the woods, and I am sorry that I will not be staying with you now. I love you," Bjorn continues, grabbing the back of Mads' head and placing a kiss on his forehead before bringing their faces together, eyes closed.

"May the dark heart of the night guide you the rest of your time on this island as it guided me last night. Until we meet again," Bjorn says before releasing Mads.

"Until we meet again, Brother," Mads replies, enclosing the black stone in his giant hand.

Mads then turns to me, saying, "Einar has lost his way since the witch whispered in his ear. There are a few Brothers you may be able to trust, but Bjorn is the only one you should listen to. Do not waste the gift of his protection. If not for yourself, then for your child."

I nod my head yes, unsure of how to respond. He looks once more at Bjorn before he begins to head slowly back up the beach towards the village.

"Mads, wait," I call, "If you find a little boy with black eyes and curly black hair, his namc is Cacl. Tell him his mother loves him. Tell him she will come back for him one day."

Mads looks at me, a sadness weighing heavily on his face. He nods and turns back around to continue his trek back.

I feel Naia move from behind my legs to the front of me. Aine's skin slides off of her, resting on my heels. Still wearing the coat of my skin, she holds on to my leg with one tiny hand, and with her other hand, she reaches an outstretched arm, the thread and whale-bone needle still dangling from it, for Bjorn. Choose the one who needs you the most, I think as I continue to watch Mads head towards the village and woods.

None of the options before me are ideal. Returning to the Sea has been unsuccessful. The village is ruined, and to take her to the wood line may mean her death. The best chance for Naia is to go with Bjorn. I don't trust him completely. It may lead to us both dying, but right now, it seems like it is our best chance. Naia, reaching out towards him, seems not the least bit afraid of him.

"We will go with you," I say, as if we have a choice, "if you promise to take care of Naia, and not let anything happen to her."

Bjorn nods yes, taking a step forward and returning Naia's reach.

We stand there in the sun, which has fully taken over the sky. The clouds seemingly part over only us, as the smoke from last night's fires have created an overcast sky over the rest of the beach. I feel the light, warm touches of the morning sun's rays on my face for what I tell myself will not be for the last time. I turn towards the Sea and see that my family has disappeared under the waves and moved beyond sight.

"Are you ready?" Bjorn asks, his large hand wrapped around Naia's tiny one.

"No," I say truthfully.

"Me either," he says, before turning towards the jetty that separates the beaches.

Naia is led by his hand as he limps slowly on his damaged leg. It's an uncomfortable sight, this large beast of a man leading my tiny daughter, still in the remains of my destroyed coat. I bend down and grab Aines' coat from the water by my feet, unsure of what to do with it at first. Not far away, her body lays in the sand, having been pushed back by the waves. I see her naked and know what I must do. I walk over to her and struggle to put her coat back on her lifeless body. After struggling to move her with my hurt hand, I finally get her covered back up. I sit there beside her, placing her face on my lap, stroking her hair before leaning down to place a kiss on her cold forehead.

"Thank you, for everything. For sacrificing yourself for me once again," I say. I gently place her head back in the sand, place my hands under her shoulders and pull. Though we are the same size, her weight is too much for me, especially after the exhaustion of last night's battles. I struggle to move her even a small distance in the sand. I try again to pull, and my feet slip as the wet sand gives way causing me to fall. As I catch my breath, I feel Bjorn's warm hand on my arm, pulling me up. Looking up into his warm, honey-colored eyes, I give in and accept his help. I watch as he gently picks her up and starts walking into the water. I grab her hand and we walk together.

"Please, let me hold her." I ask once I am chest deep in the water, knowing the Sea will help me carry her weight now.

Bjorn gently places her in my arms so that I am now cradling her, and we are rocked by the waves. I look up to the sky, then back out to the Sea, and walk us further in. I continue to move forward until my feet begin to lift from the sandy sea floor and we are floating. I take a slow, deep breath and push forward. As we rest quietly just below the waves, our hair connecting and combining in the water, moving as if alive to the pull of the currents, I give her one last kiss and let her go. I stay there, the tips of my toes barely grazing the sea floor and watch her as the currents begin to pull her out, accepting her back into our home, into the watery grave she deserves.

Shadowy outlines begin to appear as some of our family comes to take her back. My hand floats towards them and her, but they do not respond. They surround her body before gently nudging her, pushing her further into the deep, where I know they will provide her the proper send off for a matriarch.

I wish I could stay here, in the water. I give one last look around, hoping to glimpse my boys, but I see nothing. I push off and rise to the surface. Looking back towards the land, I see Bjorn and Naia waiting for me on the beach, and I begin to make my way back to them. I feel the weight of the land pulling on me as I walk out, leaving behind the weightlessness of the Sea. Each step becoming harder and heavier.

"Momma!" Naia exclaims as she runs into the shallows and into my arms, knocking me over.

"Please," Bjorn says reaching for my hand, "let me help you."

His face is rough and filled with a sadness and sorrow that is not unlike what my own face carries.

"Yes," I say, returning his reach and accepting his help fully now.

He pulls me up quickly, as if I am once again as weightless as I was in the water.

Naia reaches for him, and he scoops her back up as the three of us make our way back to the jetty barrier and to where I presume their ship lies.

We walk in silence, and it feels as though it doesn't take long at all to reach the ship.

Bjorn easily lifts me and Naia on top of the rocks before scrambling up them himself. Despite the injury to his leg, he moves swiftly and strongly, the limp not slowing him down much. The ship is unlike the fishing ones in the village; it is much larger, and covered in ornate carvings of serpent heads, giving it an ominous appearance. Bjorn walks us on board, getting us settled down in a tucked away corner in the back where a large serpent head stretches up and out from behind us.

I sit in the place Bjorn had put us, wrapped in the blankets he provided as he rummages for clothing for himself. Finding some, he sits on the bench in front of our hiding spot after dressing and begins to tend to his leg wound. Naia quickly falls asleep as I cuddle her in tightly and begin to rock us.

"Where will we go?" I ask.

"Einar will likely take us back home. From there, I will take you wherever you like." He looks up from his leg back to me, looking into my eyes and making a promise. "I will not leave you, or her, until you ask me to."

I should say thank you, show some appreciation, but all I say is, "Okay."

I am unsure how long we have been sitting there. The concept of time has been lost to me since we left the beach. I am brought out of my thoughts by the sound of men talking and walking heavy in the sand and onto the boat. Einar looks over at us as he talks to his men. Bjorn stands up as Einar addresses them, placing himself between us and them.

The men begin to file into the row of benches placed on the side of the ship as Holger hands out clothing and oars. He positions the men, moving Bjorn away from us. The ship groans as it's pushed out into the water by two other men, who quickly hop aboard with the help of the others. I look at their faces, and my sadness grows when I see that Mads is missing. I had hoped he would have changed his mind and come with us. I hope that he is okay, and that he finds some survivors as he searches. I would pray to the Sea for his safety, but I know she cannot reach him where he has gone on the land.

The ship rocks and rolls gently over the waves as we get further from shore, the beach and tree line of the woods becoming smaller in the distance. The smoke from the burned village on the cliff above the beach no longer visibly rises as the morning progresses and we stretch further away. The sun becomes hazier as we come nearer to the mist. Suddenly, Einar commands the men to hold, and the oarsmen stop rowing.

Holger gets up from his bench and comes over quickly to where Naia and I lay.

"What do you want?" I ask, trying to hide the nervousness in my voice.

"Seals can get through," he says. "We've seen them on both sides."

"No, stop!" I yell.

I fight as he rips Naia from my arms, and she cries out for me and Bjorn. Bjorn stands up and rushes over from the bench, where Holger had sat him away from us, his face full of panic and anger. Holger throws Naia at him, and before I can say or do anything. I feel Holger's rough hands on my body as I am lifted up into the air. Suddenly I feel the rush of the cold Sea water over me as I am tossed overboard and into the Sea. I struggle to get turned around in my dress, kicking up towards the surface in a panic.

"Naia!" I scream. I kick up towards the boat but am met with an oar wielded by Holger as he wears a smile, enjoying my torment.

"Stop!" I scream. "Bjorn!"

"Einar this is not the way!" I hear Bjorn roar, and as I kick up to pop up out of the water, my dress pulls me down. I can see Naia cradled in Bjorn's protective arms, looking helpless.

"This is not what you promised." I hear another voice that I don't recognize call out, though I cannot see who it belongs too.

I take a few deep breaths, willing my heart to slow down before taking one more deep breath and sinking under the water to remove my dress. I struggle to get it off, but once I do, I let it sink to the depths below. My naked body buzzes from the cold water and newfound freedom of movement. I know what it is they want from me as I surface again.

"Give me my daughter, and I will see you through," I say.

I know that Bjorn will do his best to protect her, but he is injured and outnumbered. She is still wearing her coat; it hasn't worked yet but better to be here in the water with me than in a boat full of bears. I can still see the distant shoreline of our island, and I can see my family bobbing out in the distance. I let out a shrill bark, and then another. They can help me get Naia back to shore once the men are gone.

"No, we will keep her safely here with us. Get us through the mist and we will reunite you with her. Bjorn is responsible for her until you get us through," Einar says from the middle of the boat that he commands. I look around at the men I can see from the water, and I can sense a division amongst them. Bjorn has carried Naia over to the side of the boat to better see me. His face is tense as he holds her tightly in his arms.

"Give her to me, or I will not help you pass."

Einar does not take any time to consider my words. I hear him mumble something then watch as he walks over to Bjorn and holds a sword to his throat. Bjorn growls, but with Naia in his arms there is not much he can do. Another bear man jumps up, and he is quickly pushed back down by Holger with the same oar he had used to push me back.

"Do you understand?" Einar asks me, and I do.

I turn away from the ship and work to slow my beating heart. I look to the grey sky, which is partially obscured by the mist. Taking a deep breath in, I slow the movements of my hands and legs as I lightly tread water. I try to focus on the sensation of the water around me, flowing between my fingertips and my toes. I sink a little lower into the water, with my head slightly back, only my nose and mouth remaining above surface. I take one more deep breath in and slowly sink down under the waves.

With closed eyes, I let my body free fall deeper into the Sea, asking it to accept me, to welcome me, to open up for me. I am not sure how long I allow myself to fall like this, when I finally open my eyes and look up, I can only see the vague dark shadowy outline of the ship above me. I turn to look towards the wall of mist, where I will need to find a way in this form to create an opening.

As I start to move slowly towards the mist wall, I hear the voices of my family. My sisters and brothers are swimming towards me in the safety of the deep water. I reach my hand out as they swim around me, all chattering at once. My heart starts beating faster, and I try to slow it down, but there is a sense of peace down here that I had long forgotten about, and it excites me. I close my eyes and try to calm the excitement of my heartbeat. When I open them again, my heart stops altogether.

A foot away from me are two seal pups, and I know, I know in my heart it is them. I reach for them, and the smaller one quickly places his head in my outstretched hand. I reach my other hand out, and the bigger one comes forward, placing a kiss on my face. As the pups begin to swim around my body, weaving in and around my arms and legs, I can see bright white lines on their skin that look like scars—the seams of where I had sewn my skin for them. It worked; my boys are safe. Caden and Aidan have returned to the Sea in my place.

My heart begins to feel strained, along with my lungs. My happiness and relief in this moment is being pulled at by my fear and the urgency for my daughter above. In another direction, the sorrow of my son Cael, who is lost in the woods on the island. I reach for my sons and try to pull them in, but they continue to glide around me, moving just out of reach before moving further away, back towards the colony of which they are now a part of, and my heart aches from their closeness and distance.

My lungs continue to build fire, as I have lost track of how long I have been under, and I start to swim towards the mist. The colony, sensing my task from the shadow of the boat above and my cry at the surface, begins to puff out their hoods and blow. They work together to puff and blow, creating a wave of bubbles that begins to separate the mist. They layer on top of each other in the water in a line, blowing and puffing and as the bubbles continue to move upward, the part in the mist continuing upward to the surface.

I could stay here, and let my lungs burn out, accept the salt water into them and let my body float down into the dark abyss to slumber with Aine. But Naia is still trapped on the surface. Naia still needs me. I have made many mistakes in my life, creating shame for myself and burdens to be carried. These are not the burdens of my children, but they will all carry them in some way, regardless.

Caden and Aidan now have my family and the Sea to help them bear the inheritance I have left for them. Naia will be left to bear them alone if I do not return to her. I start to kick as hard as I can. My lungs continue to burn with a fire that is running out of air to keep burning. As I come nearer to the surface, the ship begins to move away, through the opening. The harder I kick and claw my way back to the surface, the less my lungs burn, the fire fading along with my body. Darkness begins to creep around my vision. I am almost to the top. I am so close.

Naia, I am coming! I scream internally.

I reach the surface, and as my head breaks through I get one last glimpse of the ship moving swiftly beside me. A fuzzy image of a tan arm reaching for me under a light brown face and golden circle is all I see before it's all black and I am gone.

Ionna

The Kingdom
of
Einar

24

STRANGE PEOPLE IN A STRANGE LAND

I think I have been asleep for days when I finally awake safely back in the bear men's boat. My chest aches, like I have been crushed under an enormous stone. Naia lies against me, and Bjorn sits on the bench in front of where we lay.

He says one of his brothers fished me out just as the boat began to move through the break in the mist wall. That I have been unconscious until the afternoon after we had passed through the mist.

There is an uneasiness in the boat. It is clear that a break has been created amongst the bear men, though no one talks about it. There are those, like Holger, who are still dedicated to Einar and his cause, and then there are others like Bjorn, in whom I can sense a shift in the way they view their leader and their group. They are guarded, quiet.

Einar does not seem to pick up on or care about the sudden change in some of his men. He orders them about, and they follow the orders all the same. His interest in Naia only grows throughout the trip. I catch him staring at her increasingly.

He becomes more forceful in trying to engage her and me, to win our favor. My skin tingles, as if warning me of the danger that lurks each time his eyes lie upon us. I am polite when he tries to engage us. Naia refuses to look at or talk to him when he tries to talk to her. I believe she picked up on a sense of danger around him as well.

As we continue towards their land, the Sea grows agitated and the wind colder. Occasionally, I pick up on the call of one of my cousins from the deep, or catch sight of one of them breaking the surface in the distance. They all keep a wide berth around the boat, though.

I miss the Sea and my family. I miss my boys, and a part of me even misses the island and the moments it gave me watching the children and my sister Aine together. The trip is hard, and my body aches from sitting for so long in the hard, cramped space behind Bjorn's bench.

The first tiny spark of a bond between him and Naia that appeared on the beach back on the island only grows over the course of our trip. She becomes more confident and grows bolder as the days wear on. She peeks out of our hiding spot to tug on his shirt or lightly pull his hair before hiding back under the blankets he had given us to avoid being caught.

He smiles, and occasionally reaches back to give her a playful swat, making her giggle. I feel bad, but I shush her and give him a look. I didn't want to draw anymore of Einar's or Holger's attention to us than is necessary. It is mid-morning when we finally land on the rocky coast of their homeland. I am filled with relief and fear.

"Don't worry, we will slip out soon," Bjorn whispers in my ear before he jumps off the boat to help pull it in with the others.

It is snowing when we arrive on the empty beach. There is no party there to greet us, which is a relief. We wait patiently for Bjorn to come and get us off the boat. Naia climbs up on Bjorn's bench to cautiously peek over the side of the boat at the strange new land. It is heavily wooded and dark. The trees are thick and tall like an imposing fortress meant to keep people out. I feel uneasy, looking at them. I had not been afraid of the woods back on the island, but these seem much darker and ominous. After what feels like forever, Bjorn finally came to retrieve us from the boat.

"Stay close," he warns.

As if I would wander away from him, our only source of protection amongst these men and this land. A trust has formed between us during the journey. I know I will never again fully trust or rely on anyone besides myself, but with Bjorn, I am coming close.

The men make camp at the tree line of the beach that we had landed on. Fires are made, and a few of the men are sent into the woods to forage for dinner. Naia and I stay close to the shelter that Bjorn had made for us with some of the furs on the boat and fallen limbs from the trees. I try to keep her hidden, out of Einar's view. Despite my best attempts, she wriggles free and runs out to stretch her legs, which had been cramped for so long during the boat ride.

One of her successful escape attempts leads us right into Einar, who grabs her by her arms and squats down to be eye level with her. Naia freezes, along with my heart, as he stares into her big, black eyes with his piercing blue ones, searching for something inside her as he holds her in his grasp. I run forward and grab Naia, breaking his grasp on her tiny shoulders as I scoop her up in my arms.

"It's not safe to be running about near the woods," he says, still looking at Naia. "It's filled with monsters and witches that would happily eat up a small girl, and her mother." He turns his gaze to me, then erupts into an unsettling laugh.

"We have heard that before," I say in response as I quickly take Naia back to the shelter Bjorn had made us.

"Naia, you can't run off like that. You must stay here out of view with me for a while longer, ok?" I tell Naia, pleading with her to listen.

The sun begins to lower and Kare, a kind, light-haired bear man, brings us some meat that they had caught and smoked over the fire.

"It won't be long now," he says.

I am not sure what he means, but I take the meat and thank him. The men continue to work around the camp. A large tent is made for Einar, and he calls the men in to gather as Naia and I are left alone in our shelter, protected by the warmth of the fire that Bjorn had built for us. With a full belly, Naia begins to fall asleep, and I fight the urge to do the same, but am unsuccessful as I feel myself falling asleep.

An owl hoots loudly, waking me up. I feel beside me for my daughter, but do not find her.

"Momma," she calls, and I look up to see that Naia is standing under the peaceful moon, waiting for me at the tree line.

I get up, take her hand, and we enter the woods together. I no longer fear the woods. There is a sense of safety and familiarity in them now that wasn't there before as we walk a well-worn path that I had not noticed before. I look down at Naia and see her sweet, round face looking up at mine and smiling. We continue down the path until we enter a clearing with a large, dark, stone altar in the center of it.

"Mama, look," Naia says, pointing to a giant bear skull that lay on a bear skin fur on top of the smooth stone altar. It's as white as the whalebone needle that I still carry with me.

"Do you like it?" A woman's voice says softly to us.

I look around the clearing and see a beautiful woman with dark red lips slip out from the woods and come to stand next to the altar. Her hair is black like ours, but it flows straight from her head down her body, not wild like the wind and waves like ours. She wears a dress the color of the sea waves churning in a storm. It is adorned with tiny rocks as beautiful as sea glass, and it glows like the poisonous algae does when the water becomes too warm in the sea. Beautiful and dangerous.

"Don't be scared," she says in a musical voice that echoes slightly as she comes closer to us.

"Look," she says, pointing up to the sky above us. "Isn't it beautiful?"

The same smokey lights that I saw outside my house the night the bear men came are once again dancing beautifully in the sky. I pick up Naia, and as she reaches her hand up to the sky, the lights begin to descend downwards to us. I look at Naia and smile, then reach my hand up towards the light along with her. As the lights continue to dance towards us, I feel a warmth growing around us.

"It's time," the woman says.

"Wake up!" Bjorn's voice comes crashing through the clearing and from inside my head.

Everything is dark. The woman, the clearing, the lights, they are all gone. My chest hurts, and I feel rough hands shaking me as I struggle to open my eyes. Certain parts of my body feel numb as I struggle to sit up. Once I gain my consciousness back, I panic and begin to feel around for Naia. I take a deep breath in and can let it out when I feel her warm body laying not far from mine.

"It's time," Bjorn says quietly, pulling me to standing.

I look around and see the light brown-haired man standing outside our shelter, along with a blonde-haired, heavily-bearded one.

"It's okay, they are with us," Bjorn assures me.

He then gently picks up Naia, who remains asleep, and motions for me to follow him back to the boat, where Kare is already waiting. I look at Bjorn questioningly as he hands Naia to Kare and then quickly lifts me up inside as well. Silently, Bjorn and the other two men push the boat as quietly as they can into the water before Kare helps each one climb in.

"Where are we going?" I ask Bjorn quietly.

"Someplace that Einar will not expect," he says.

"What if they wake up?" I whisper urgently.

"They won't. Not for a while anyway. Gunnar," he says pointing to the blonde-haired man with the beard, "found some roots in the woods and put it in the remaining mead we had onboard."

We continue on the boat along the shoreline before the men divert it down a large river going inward towards the land and woods. I bring Naia back to our hiding spot from the previous journey and settle her back in on my lap. I look up at the moon and stars, and I see a faint, smokey light dancing up above and I think to myself, *isn't it beautiful?*

25

GLOSSARY

Below you will find a list of terms and how they are used in this story which may differ from the original meaning in order to fit the story.

Selkie - In Celtic and Norse mythology, a Selkie is a mythological being that takes the form of a seal. However, it can transform into a human by shedding its "coat" or seal skin.

Hamingja - A female light guardian who is the embodiment of the northern lights. She represents your success in life, and possession of her can be passed down or borrowed by others.

Hamr - Refers to your physical appearance which could also be manipulated for shape shifting.

Hammrammr - The ability to shapeshift.

Hugr- Your personality or character.

Rán -A Sea goddess.

Bára - One of the nine daughters of the Sea god and his wife Rán.

Volva - A Norse witch or prophetess.

The Washerwoman – A type of banshee. She is a messenger from the otherworld and an omen of death.

JKDIVIA